D1605685

PUZZLE HOUSE

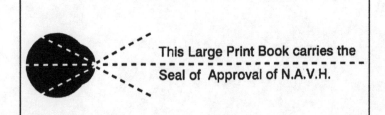

This Large Print Book carries the
Seal of Approval of N.A.V.H.

PUZZLE HOUSE

LILLIAN DUNCAN

THORNDIKE PRESS
A part of Gale, a Cengage Company

Farmington Hills, Mich • San Francisco • New York • Waterville, Maine
Meriden, Conn • Mason, Ohio • Chicago

Copyright © 2017 by Lillian Duncan.
All scripture quotations, unless otherwise indicated, are taken from the Holy Bible, New International Version®, NIV®, Copyright 1973, 1978, 1984, 2011 by Biblica, Inc.™ Used by permission of Zondervan. All rights reserved worldwide. www.zondervan.com
Thorndike Press, a part of Gale, a Cengage Company.

LIBRARY OF CONGRESS CIP DATA ON FILE.
CATALOGUING IN PUBLICATION FOR THIS BOOK
IS AVAILABLE FROM THE LIBRARY OF CONGRESS

978-1-4328-5145-3 (hardcover)

Published in 2018 by arrangement with Pelican Ventures, LLC

Printed in Mexico
1 2 3 4 5 6 7 22 21 20 19 18

This and all I do is for God's Glory.

To my amazing husband,
Ronny, without you my stories
wouldn't get written.
Thanks for all that you do.

To all those who suffer from
Neurofibromatosis of any type. Life can
be difficult but with God all things are
possible, even peace and joy.

1

"I hate you." Nia's gaze shot little darts of anger at the woman standing by the car door.

The woman met her gaze with a smile.

Which infuriated Nia even more. "I said I hate you and I do."

"You don't hate me. You're just angry." Her voice remained calm, almost emotionless.

"Don't you care about me, Auntie?"

"I'm not going to dignify that question with an answer." She leaned down. "Are you ready?"

"I said don't you care about me? Why are you making me do this?"

"Because I do love you so very much." One of her hands moved under Nia, the other moved to her back.

Nia knocked her hands away. "I can do it myself. If I wanted to. I'm not going in there. You can't make me."

"I would think you had better ways to use the little bit of energy you have than arguing with me about this. We agreed."

"No, *we* didn't." Her lip trembled. No crying. Crying wouldn't change anything. She flopped back against the car seat, exhausted. "I never wanted to come and you know it."

Her aunt knelt down beside her, eyes filled with tears. "Please. This will be a good thing, Nia. I promise."

"How do you know that?"

"I can't explain it but I know it will be. If you just give it half a chance. Please."

"What if I say no?"

Her aunt's head drooped.

No one spoke.

When her aunt gazed back at her, there was no pity in her eyes, only strength. Her shoulders moved back ever so slightly. "You'll still have to stay."

"So I got no choice."

"Nope. None at all."

"That ain't right, Auntie."

"I'm sure it seems that way to you. But I'm the one responsible for you. So it's my decision. I love you and I have to do what I think is right."

"I hate you."

Her aunt patted her cheek. "I hear you,

sweetie." She leaned in and scooped Nia up. A moment later Nia was in the wheelchair she hated almost as much as her disease. As her aunt wheeled her toward the house, Nia wiped away tears. She couldn't help but stare at her surroundings, so different from her life in the city.

This place had more grass than her whole neighborhood. And a pond and trees and a barn. A barn? She'd never seen a barn in real life before — only in pictures and on TV. Were there really animals in it?

The house was pretty in a country hick sort of way. A long porch wrapped around both sides and there were a bunch of rocking chairs lined up. Two of the rockers had a small table with a checker set between them. How old-fashioned could you get? Still it was sort of pretty. "Where's my welcoming committee, Auntie? I would have thought they'd be thrilled I was coming."

Her aunt patted her shoulder. "They are thrilled. I guess we should use the ramp." She made a sudden turn and pushed Nia toward the ramp at the far side of the porch.

When they got to the door, Nia's aunt stopped. "I don't see a doorbell. Think we should just walk in?"

"Don't see why not."

"Maybe we should knock?"

Nia leaned forward, grabbed the knob and then opened the door. She looked back at her aunt with a grin. "Too late."

Her aunt *tsked* as she pushed the wheelchair into the house. A huge sign hung on the wall.

WELCOME TO THE PUZZLE HOUSE
And now these three remain: faith, hope and love.
But the greatest of these is love.

"Yea, whatevs." Nia mumbled.

To their right there was a large room. There was a white boy sitting at a table totally focused on something on the surface.

An old white lady — older than dirt — sat in a chair in front of the largest picture window Nia had ever seen.

She was whispering with another white lady, not as old

Nia's aunt pushed her and the chair into the room.

No one noticed them.

"Ain't nobody going to notice the sick girl in the wheelchair?" Nia asked.

The woman standing by the old white lady turned. "Oh, my goodness. I didn't hear you come in. Of course there's lots of things I can't hear these days." She hurried toward them but then stumbled and fell forward.

10

Rachel grabbed onto the nearest table and righted herself. "Oops. I know better than to rush. I don't know what I was thinking."

"Are you all right?" The woman pushing the wheelchair asked.

"Fine and dandy." She took a deep breath and walked toward them. Much slower this time. "I'm Rachel and you must be Margaretta and Nia. It's so wonderful to meet both of you. Welcome to The Puzzle House."

"Yea, whatevs." Nia mumbled, clearly not happy to be here.

"I wasn't expecting you for another few hours."

"We got an earlier start than planned." Margaretta stepped out from behind the wheel chair. "I'm Nia's aunt. We talked on the phone. Margaretta Johnson."

Ignoring the outstretched hand, Rachel moved closer and enveloped her in a hug. "It's nice to meet you Margaretta. Finally. Though I'm sorry it's under these circumstances."

A momentary stiffness, then Margaretta relaxed in the hug. When she stepped back she smiled as if they were old friends. She wiped a tear. "I guess I should thank you.

Not just for accepting Nia but for . . . other things."

"No thanks needed. I'm just so happy to meet you and your beautiful niece."

Nia was staring at the two of them with a confused expression. Good. A little curiosity could make the week go a little easier.

"What are you thanking her for? For taking me off your hands?" Nia's tone said she wasn't in the mood for niceties. "She —"

"Nia, be nice. This is a very special woman and we are very blessed to be here."

"I ain't nothing and I'm sure not blessed. I don't wanna be here with her. I want to go home. With you."

"I'm sorry, but that won't happen, sweetie. I promise I'll be back in a week. But for now this is where you need to be, Nia." She looked up at Rachel. "I'm really sorry. She's . . . having a difficult day."

Rachel smiled at Nia. She was so thin, probably not more than ninety pounds. Her brown face was gaunt. She had only a bit of hair on her head, mostly bald from the chemo, no doubt. But in spite of all that, she was truly beautiful. "Don't worry about it, Margaretta. It's such a blessing to have Nia here with me. I'm looking forward to spending some time with her."

A choking sound came out of Nia's mouth

but she said nothing.

"Well, I hope Nia listens to —"

"Listens? What that old white lady gonna teach me about my life? She don't know nothing about me."

"Nia. Don't be rude. We don't talk about people by their colors." Her aunt looked horrified and embarrassed all at the same time. "We don't like that when people judge us that way."

Nia met Rachel's gaze for the first time. "Sorry. No offense meant."

"None taken."

"See, Auntie. She don't care that I noticed she's white." She looked at Rachel. "So, what you think you gonna teach me that I don't already know?"

A challenge? That was good. Much better to be angry than apathetic. Just as it said in Revelation, better to be hot or cold than lukewarm. There was nothing about this young girl that was lukewarm.

"Is that a challenge, Nia? If it is, it's not one I'm taking. What you learn or don't learn here at The Puzzle House will be up to you, my dear." She looked at Nia's aunt. "Don't worry about us, we'll be fine. Won't we, Nia?"

"Whatevs."

Margaretta took a moment to glare at Nia

but smiled when she looked at Rachel. "I'll go get her luggage."

The boy at the table jumped up. "Not necessary. That's my job."

"Oh. Thank you so much."

His curly brown hair flopped in his eyes. He brushed it away. His blue eyes twinkled with curiosity as he looked at Nia.

Rachel was glad Brandon was here this week. The two of them could keep each other company. "Hi. I'm Brandon."

"What do I . . ." Her aunt's hand touched Nia's shoulder. Nia rolled her eyes. "I'm Nia."

"Nia. That's an awesome name. What's it mean?"

"How should I know? Probably means sick girl with no hair." She touched the top of her head to emphasize her point.

"Probably not. I didn't even notice it." He turned his attention to Margaretta. "Do I need the keys?"

Margaretta nodded and handed him the keys. "The luggage is in the trunk."

"Great. I'll be right back."

True to his promise, he walked back in with two suitcases. Margaretta took the smaller of the suitcases. "Nia isn't on any . . . treatment right now. She has a few meds to . . . help keep her comfortable. I've

14

made a list of what and when she's allowed to take them. The others are just vitamins which she will take every day, right Nia?"

"Sure, Auntie." The words were correct, the tone was not. "Whatevs."

Rachel had figured that Nia would be a handful after several conversations with Margaretta. Most of the people who came to The Puzzle House wanted to be there. "I'll keep the one with the meds."

"Why? I can take care of 'em myself." Nia's hands went to her hips in spite of being in the wheelchair. "Don't need you checking up on me. I can take care of myself. I don't need nobody to help me."

"I'm sure that's very true, but unless you're eighteen, I have to take care of the meds. Rules are rules. So not much point in arguing about it." Rachel turned to Margaretta. "You're welcome to spend as much time as you'd like with us. Even stay overnight if you choose. We've got the room."

"I'd love to but I can't. If I leave now I can get back home by bedtime. Work tomorrow, you know." Her arms went around the young girl. "I love you, Nia. Please understand. This is where you need to be right now."

"I won't understand. I don't want to understand. I need to be home so I can die

15

in peace. Not here with strangers. Don't leave me."

Margaretta touched Nia's chin and gazed into the young girl's eyes. "You will not die this week. I promise you that."

"I might as well. Since you're leaving me. What do I care what happens to me? You don't."

"I'm not abandoning you, Nia, and you know it."

"Sure feels like you are."

"Stop trying to make me feel guilty. Please, trust me. This will be a great experience for you. If . . ." Margaretta's chin quivered. "If you give it a chance."

"I don't want to die here. Alone. Without you."

Margaretta stood up and straightened her shoulders. "I will see you next week. I love you, sweetie. Have a wonderful time."

Nia's anger dissolved. "Please, Auntie. Don't make me stay here. I want to be home with you. And my friends. And Cubbie."

"And you will be soon, but not right now." She knelt down in front of Nia once again. "You trust me, don't you?"

Nia nodded.

"Then trust me this time. This is the place you need to be for now. If you . . . if you . . ." She sighed, and then stood up. "Just trust me on this. Enjoy the week here with Rachel. Think of it as a vacation."

"A vacation in the middle of nowhere." She glared at Rachel. "With nobody I want to be with. Sounds like a lot of fun."

"Gotta go, sweetie." Tears were in Margaretta's voice as she walked out of the room.

Nia gave Rachel a militant look. "What? The sick girl gotta carry her own suitcase to her room?"

Brandon moved closer. "That's my job. I'll take it up for you and set it on your bed." He looked at Rachel. "I'll be back later."

"And I'll show you around while he does that." Rachel pushed the wheelchair toward the door. "Let's take that tour now."

"Let's not. I don't need this thing when I'm in the house." Nia stood up. She touched the wheelchair. "I hate this thing. But I get so tired sometimes. Especially when I walk. I guess that's why Auntie wanted to make sure I had it with me."

"I understand. The good thing is there's plenty of room here for it. Use it when you want. Sort of like this cane. I use it sometimes but not all the time." Rachel showed Nia the cane leaning on the wall.

"Why do you need a cane? You sick too?"

17

"Balance issues. I get sort of wobbly sometimes. The cane keeps me from falling down. Most of the time."

"Oh great! Sick girl in a wheelchair and an old white woman who falls down." She paused. "No offense meant."

"None taken. I see you still have your sense of humor. Nia."

"Yeah, whatevs."

"Nia, I'm not your enemy."

"Didn't say you were."

"There's no reason we can't be friends." Rachel looped her arm through Nia's and led her out of the room. "Who's Cubbie?"

"My cat. But she doesn't know she's a cat. She thinks she's tough, like a bear. That's why I call her Cubbie."

"She sounds like a great cat. We don't have any cats in the house because of my allergies. But a few cats hang around outside. So, welcome to The Puzzle House."

They were in a hallway. The staircase was in the middle with closed doors on each side of it. A lift was against one wall of the stairs.

Nia pointed at it. "I suppose I have to use that thing."

"Only if you want. It's easy enough to use. Sit down in it, buckle up, and then hit the button." Rachel moved to the room to the left. There were several chairs and two sofas

18

in the room. "This is the meeting room."

"We gotta have meetings?"

Rachel laughed. "Not really. But meetings can be helpful to keep things running smoothly. It's really a quiet room in the house. To read or study or just relax."

"Quiet. This whole place is quiet. Too quiet. How many people are here now?"

"There's you, of course. And you met Brandon. Annie's the older woman I was talking with when you came in. That's all. We have enough rooms for six guests."

Rachel closed the door the meeting room. "You've already been in the puzzle room. We'll come back to that in a minute. Let me show you the kitchen and eating area."

They made their way to a huge room. The kitchen took up one side and a large table filled the other space. The walls were made of wood planks with lots of dark holes. On the other side of the room was a huge picnic style table.

"Kind of cool. What do you call that?" Nia pointed at the walls.

"Knotty pine. I like it too." Rachel walked to a large refrigerator. "Anything in this one is yours to eat whenever you get hungry. The other one has the ingredients for the meals so it's better if you don't eat from that one." Puzzle House

"Don't matter. I don't get very hungry any more. The doctors said it's my body shutting down."

Rachel walked over and patted her. "I'm sorry. Let me take you back to the puzzle room and then you'll probably want to rest some. Are you tired?"

"A little."

The puzzle room was empty. One side had large windows that showcased a beautiful pond, and trees, now showing their fall colors. In front of the windows were a sofa and several chairs arranged in a semi-circle with a coffee table. In the middle of the room were card tables, each with two chairs.

"What's with the tables?"

"Well, we aren't called The Puzzle House for no reason. Every guest works on a puzzle while they're here. The tables are the perfect size for the puzzles."

"I ain't never worked on no puzzle." Nia glared at her. "And I don't plan on wasting time doin' one now. Where's the TV?"

"No TVs here. At least not for guests. I have one in my room so I can keep up with the news from time to time. And the weather reports."

"I can't watch TV?"

"Sorry."

Nia rolled her eyes. "I'm gonna be so bored."

"That's why we have the puzzles."

"I already said I don't want to do no puzzle."

"I'm sorry I thought I heard you say you weren't going to do a puzzle." She lifted her hair to reveal a hearing aid, but I'm sure I heard wrong." Rachel met her glare with what she hoped was calmness. "Besides it's a rule. The only one we have, actually. Well, that and respecting each other, which is not really a rule. Just common courtesy."

"Whatcha going to do if I don't do no puzzle? Send me home?" Nia's hand went to her hip as she glared at Rachel.

Rachel said nothing, just held Nia's gaze. Waiting.

Nia threw up her hands. "Fine. Where's mine?"

"Just like in life, you get to make your own choice. Pick the one you want." Rachel motioned at a shelf across the room.

"Ain't nothing about my life, I got to pick. You think I picked my mama to be a druggie? You think I picked to get sick? You think I picked to be dying? You think I even picked to be here?"

"I suppose not. And you're right; we don't always get to pick our circumstances. But there are still choices we all get to make. And those choices can make a big difference in the life we live."

She rolled her eyes. "Yeah, whatevs."

Nia walked to the puzzle shelf with attitude.

"The puzzles go from easy to super hard. Left to right."

Nia walked to the easy section.

Rachel smiled and waited.

"Ain't you going to tell me not to pick the easiest?"

"You get to pick whatever one you want."

Nia picked up a box, stood there contemplating, and then set it back down. After squaring her shoulders, her chin jutted. Then she walked to the opposite side of the shelf. "You know it'd be a lot easier to pick one if I could see what it looked like." She pointed at the plain brown boxes. "Most puzzle boxes have the picture on them."

"Sort of like life, huh? It would be a lot easier if we could see the finished picture. But we only get to live our life one piece at a time. It's only later that we see how one piece fits into another piece."

"I 'spose so. Well, I don't think I should pick the super hard since I never did no puzzle before."

"Up to you, my dear."

22

"I bet you thought I'd pick the really easy ones. Like I was a chicken or something."

"I don't think you're a chicken. I think you're quite brave. But if you'd picked the easy one that would have been fine. God seems to have a way of matching the person up with the right puzzle for them."

"Yeah, whatevs." Nia ran her hand over several boxes, picked one up and shook it, then set it back on the shelf. She picked up another, shook it. "This sounds like the right one to me."

Rachel sat down at one of the tables in silent invitation.

Nia set the box down, but didn't open it. "So are you a nurse or something?"

"No, I'm not."

"Well, isn't that what this is? A place to die? One of those hospice places where people go when they're going to die. The doc said I'm done. No more treatment. Nothing else they can do for me. Time for me to go home and die. I don't think Auntie wants me to die in her house so she brought me here. That way I can't haunt her. The doctor said it's all up to me now."

"And up to God."

Nia sputtered at the word. "God. What's He got to do with anything?"

"Everything." Rachel smiled.

23

"Yea, whatevs." Nia shrugged. "Don't make no difference one way or the other to God what happens to me. He don't care nothing about me."

"Is that what you really believe, Nia?"

Another shrug. Then she picked up the puzzle box, giving it an angry shake. "I still don't know why there ain't no picture on the box. I mighta picked an ugly one."

"There are no ugly puzzles."

Nia gave her an assessing look.

"See all the beautiful puzzles on the walls?" Rachel motioned with her hand.

Under each puzzle was a picture of the person who'd put it together, some had two or three pictures beneath them.

"Didn't notice them." Her gaze moved around the room as she studied the puzzles. "I didn't know they made so many different puzzles."

"Every puzzle at The Puzzle House is unique. Just as each of our guests are."

"You gonna put mine up there after I die?"

"Who says you'll die?"

"The doctors. And Auntie, when she thinks I'm not listening."

"Don't believe everything you hear. It's still up to God, no matter what the doctors say."

"Well God sure ain't listening to me. If

24

He was, I wouldn't be here. With you."

Rachel smiled again. "Are you sure about that?"

Instead of answering, Nia picked up the puzzle box and poured out the pieces. She stared at them. "What a mess. I ain't ever going to get this thing together. I shoulda picked an easier one."

Rachel smiled. "Too late now. Unless you want to give up?"

Nia's chin jutted out and her voice became defiant. "I don't give up."

"Are you sure about that? Because it sounds as if you've given up on living to me. You've decided you'll die because the doctors said so. They aren't always right, you know."

Ignoring Rachel, Nia picked up two pieces and stared at them. "I'm pretty sure I can't do this."

"Giving up isn't allowed here at The Puzzle House."

"Another rule? Thought you only had one."

"Mmm . . . you're right. I guess there are a few more than I realized. But don't panic over the puzzle. Concentrate on one piece at a time, my dear. That's all we ever have to do."

"Isn't that what they say about druggies?

One day at a time. Besides I don't got all that many days left. I'm pretty sure this puzzle ain't getting put together." Nia pointed at the wall behind Rachel. "You got any puzzles of yours up there?"

"I've done a few over the years. But I don't display them. I put these up to help me remember my friends."

"Cause all of them died."

"Not all. Some died and some are still alive. But we all have to die sometime. It's a part of life. And it's not always in the way we expect." She stood up and walked over to a puzzle. "Take this one. Monique survived her cancer, only to be killed in a car accident ten years later."

Nia walked up beside her. "Kinda makes me think it's just not worth it. What's the point? If you're just going to die, anyway. You know what I mean?"

"I see what you mean, but every life has a point. Just ask Monique's children, who had their mother for ten more precious years. One's a teacher and one's a doctor now. In those ten years, Monique not only got to watch them grow up, but she had the opportunity to teach them what they needed to learn so they could help the people they're helping now."

"But she still died."

26

"Dying is part of life. That doesn't mean that every life isn't valuable. No matter how short or how long."

"Nothing valuable about me. Just ask my Mama. She wouldn't give up the drugs for me."

"My dear, you couldn't be more wrong. You're more valuable than you know." Rachel patted her arm. "God loves you so very much and has great plans for you. That's one of His promises."

"Great plans? Like what in the next two weeks or so? Maybe a month if I'm lucky." Nia shrugged off Rachel's hand. She motioned at the puzzles. "I 'spose you want me to think you remember all these people and their puzzles."

"I do remember them. They weren't just guests at The Puzzle House, they became my friends. I care about them and their lives."

Nia took several steps and pointed at a puzzle. "Tell me about this one." Her gaze held a challenge as she covered up the picture below it.

Probably only the first of many tests. Rachel looked at the puzzle. "That's Mount McKinley. That puzzle was done by a young man named Tommy. Interestingly enough, he now lives in Alaska with his wife and three children."

"Why is that interesting?"

"Mount McKinley's in Alaska. After Tommy finished his puzzle, he decided to take a trip there and that's where he met his wife. That's what I mean about God helping you to pick the perfect puzzle."

Nia shrugged. "Probably just a coincidence."

"If you say so, but I don't believe in coincidences. What most people call coincidences is God working in our lives."

"Don't know about that since he never did nothing for me." Nia muttered as she walked back to the table and sat down. She stared at the puzzle pieces.

Rachel hid a smile at the look of determination that crossed Nia's face. Rachel allowed the girl a few minutes and recalled warm memories of her guests as she looked at the puzzles gracing the wall.

The girl settled in, sorting pieces, calming as she became involved in the task.

Rachel took the seat opposite Nia.

"So if this place ain't a hospice, what is it?"

"It's my home."

"What's that got to do with me? Why did all those people come here? Why am I here?"

"To work on your puzzle, of course."

"That don't make no sense to me. You really are a strange white lady." She paused. "No offense."

"None taken, dear. I agree with you. I am a little strange." She grinned at Nia. "Or maybe a lot. It depends on the day, I guess. It's sort of the same with puzzles. They often don't make sense. You can't figure anything out, and then you add one piece and it all makes so much more sense."

Nia said nothing. She scooted two pieces toward each other. Picking up one, she placed it into the other. With a slight smile, she held them up. "Look, they fit."

"So they do. Puzzles can be solved if you take the time and don't give up."

"Auntie keeps telling me to not give up. But . . ." Her eyes filled with tears. Then she took a deep breath and shook her head. "What's your obsession with puzzles anyway?"

"Not an obsession, just a way to help me make sense of life."

"You don't look like you need any help. You seem like you know what you're doing. Got this nice house and a pond. You must be rich."

"Oh, we all need help. Me most of all. An interesting thing about puzzles is they aren't really meant to be done all alone. Some people prefer that, of course, but it's a lot more fun when you let others help. And that's where I come in."

"I 'spose. So what did you need help with?"

"Many, many things. A long time ago, I thought I knew everything I needed to know. And then I found out I didn't know anything. Want to hear about it?"

"I guess that's why I'm here. You get to talk and I gotta listen."

"Only if you want to, my sweet Nia."

"It's not like I got anything else to do." She bit down on her lip as if thinking over the options. "You gonna help me with my puzzle if I let you talk?"

"Sure I can do that." Rachel began to turn the puzzle pieces colored side up. "So here's what happened . . ."

2

It was typical of her days. Too many things to do in too short of a time. Rachel's heels clicked on the linoleum tiles as she rushed down the hall, even as her mind checked off the next three errands on her list. Oh, well, this was why she'd taken the promotion at Global Entertainment. She'd earned it with her ability to get a hundred things done at once. She had no intention of letting her boss down.

In spite of the horrible weather, her first conference was only three days away. She hoped she would get everything done in time. Of course, she had assistants, and they were good, but it was up to her to make sure everything was just perfect. Even if that meant no sleep until the conference was over. She didn't want to just pass this test, she wanted an A plus.

Rachel peered out the window as she buttoned up her coat and pulled on gloves. A world of ice and snow awaited. The weatherman was predicting sunshine for the day of the conference, but it was hard to imagine on this dismal day.

She'd lived in the South her whole life. This was her first winter experience in the North. Unfortunately, accepting her dream job meant living up in this frozen tundra.

"Night, Mrs. Summers." Martha said as she passed her.

"Going home early?" The moment the words were out Rachel regretted them, they sounded petty and recriminating.

Martha's face flushed red. "Dan told us all to go home. Because of the storm. He didn't want us driving home later when it would be even worse."

"Of course, I didn't mean it like that. Just making conversation. See you tomorrow, Martha. Drive carefully." The frigid wind slapped Rachel's face as she followed Martha out. Even though it was mid-afternoon, it seemed more like evening. Rachel stepped carefully onto the icy lower step. Her foot slipped. Her purse and briefcase went flying as she grabbed for the railing and her back slammed into the concrete steps. Pain shot down her spine. A small scream escaped. Rachel lay there, too stunned to move, pain radiating in too many places to accurately assess. Cold wetness seeped through her coat and her clothes. She rolled, hands flopping, trying to get back up.

Martha knelt beside her. "Are you all right, Mrs. Summers?"

Rachel nodded, too shaken to speak. She managed to sit up. The wetness had probably ruined her new suit.

"You don't look all right. Maybe I should call an ambulance?"

Rachel forced a smile. "That's not necessary, I'll live." She stood and ran her hand down the leg of her pants. "Not so sure about this suit, though. It's the first time I've worn it."

"It's beautiful. I meant to tell you that earlier, but you were so busy. I didn't want to bother you."

No wonder she hadn't made any real friends yet. Her coworkers thought they'd bother her. She needed to be more approachable. "Thanks, Martha. And please call me Rachel."

Martha's smile could've brightened a room. "I love the color of your suit, Rachel. It's the perfect shade of green for your complexion. Are you sure you're not hurt?"

"Just my dignity."

"Well, go home and get into a warm pair of jammies, put your feet up and relax.

You've earned it. You work way too hard. You make the rest of us seem downright lazy."

"Sounds wonderful, but I can't. I'm on my way to the arena for a meeting to firm up the last minute details."

"They can wait until tomorrow, Mrs. Sum . . . Rachel. Dan was clear. He wanted us all to go home before the weather gets any worse. I know he meant you, too."

"Well, it's practically on my way home anyway. I promise I'll go home as soon as I check in with them. In fact, it will be nice to spend a long evening at home with Cooper. He's my husband." She picked up her purse and the briefcase. "I might even cook dinner. That is if I remember how. It's been so long."

The two separated as they approached Rachel's car.

Martha turned back. "Be careful driving home. You're not used to driving in this snow and ice yet. It can be really tricky."

"Good advice that I certainly plan on taking. See you tomorrow." Rachel slid into her seat and turned the ignition. Waiting for the car to warm, she willed her nerves to calm. She waved to several more people as she waited for the jitters to subside.

Putting the car in gear, she cautiously

drove to the highway exit ramp. "I'll never get used to driving in this slushy mess."

Get over to the arena, check on the final details, and then head home. Another forty minute drive — in good weather. Probably an extra hour in this snow.

Cooper had insisted on a more rural setting to live in, one she'd readily agreed to. How many husbands would cheerfully pull up roots so a wife could have her dream job? They had trees, a garden, and a small pond. Cooper loved it.

She hadn't had much time to make their new house into a real home. Guilt tugged at her. She hadn't had much time at home at all lately.

But Cooper never complained so he must be happy. Even as she thought the words, she knew it wasn't true. As much as she loved her job, she loved Cooper more and needed to show him, something she'd not done much of lately.

The highway was clogged with commuters heading home early because of the weather. She should take Martha's advice — and she would, right after her meeting.

A pick-up passed so close the car shook.

"Slow down!" she yelled.

The truck cut her off as he maneuvered in front of her. She fought the urge to hit the

35

brake, which was the wrong thing to do according to the Driving-In-Ice class she'd taken. Inch by inch, Rachel made her way toward the ramp.

Why hadn't she been happy with the job she'd had? It had been a perfectly good job, but she always had to be moving up to the next level. She'd gotten the call she'd worked for her whole career and jumped at the opportunity.

Vice-president in charge of conferences for Global Entertainment. The big time. They produced conferences all over the country. Of course, she only worked on conferences here in Cleveland, but that could change in the future. She had to prove herself first. Which was why everything had to be perfect for the upcoming conference.

She'd left Georgia, where a winter storm warning meant an inch or two of snow that would melt in a day or so. "But no, I had to move to where the action was." She glared at the snow still coming down. "No one to blame but myself."

The traffic started moving once again.

She should have called before she left the office to let the people at the meeting know she was on her way. Oh well, too late now. Taking her foot off the brake, she made a right turn. Her heart stopped.

A semi skidded, coming straight at her. The cars on either side of the truck swerved away from the out-of-control vehicle. The truck swayed one way and then the other.

Without thought, Rachel slammed on the brakes. Her car spun in dizzying circles, but she could still see the truck, its jack-knifed trailer heading directly towards her. She squeezed her eyes shut, heart in her throat, terror filling her mind. "Oh, noooo . . .".

Rachel opened her eyes. She was late. The meeting! Why was she laying here? Memory took several long moments to surface. Snow. Ice. Truck. Wait, it must not have hit her. She didn't feel any pain. In fact, she'd never felt better in her life. So where was she and why was she here? She glanced around.

A man stood in front of her surrounded by a light so bright she couldn't see his face. No doctors or nurses. No equipment. Surely something must be seriously wrong with her. One didn't hit a semi-truck head on and walk away from it.

Maybe she'd slid out of the way at the last second and passed out from the terror. But if she hadn't hit the truck, why couldn't she remember? Must be a head injury.

The man stepped closer, his features came into focus, but the brightness followed him.

As her gaze connected with his, all her questions were forgotten. A warmth settled in her heart. No fear or worry. Only peace. A wonderful sweet peace.

He smiled at her.

She smiled back.

He couldn't be the doctor. Instead of a suit or scrubs, he had on a . . . she squinted to get her eyes to focus. Because obviously, she was seeing things. The man had on a robe — like from Bible times. She must have really hit her head.

"My dear sweet Rachel."

As He said her name, a tingle went down her spine. She opened her mouth but no words came out. Her heart filled with . . . impossible. Finally, she managed to utter a single word. "Jesus?"

"Yes." The smile made His face glow even more.

"Did I die?"

"No."

"Am I going to die?"

"Of course, everyone dies sometime. But this is not your day. I don't want to talk about dying, I want to talk about living."

She definitely must have a head injury. But it didn't matter. Jesus was here. Standing in front of her — smiling at her. Amazing! If it was an hallucination, it was OK with her.

"It's not a dream or an hallucination. I'm here. I'm real. Just as I promised, I am with you always." He held out his hand. "Would you like to take a walk with Me?"

When their fingers touched, she gasped. "My Lord, my Savior. I . . . I . . . I . . ." She couldn't find the words to express her feelings.

"I love you, too, Rachel. Ready to take that walk?"

"If you think I can."

"Of course, you can. My strength will be your strength. I am with you as I always will be."

So much . . . love. Joy. And more. There were no words to describe it.

She floated out of bed and looked down.

Doctors and nurses surrounded her body. Blood streaked her face. Orders were being yelled as a doctor stuck a tube of some sort in her mouth.

"Wow. It looks like I really got hurt."

"What do you expect when a semi plows into you?" He chuckled.

And she did the same. "I've always been afraid of semis."

"I know."

"I always knew one of them would be the death of me. It looks like I was right."

39

"Things are not always what they seem, my sweet Rachel."

"That looks pretty clear to me." She pointed down at her very broken body. Then she touched His cheek. "But You're here, with me. I must be having one of those near-death experiences, right?"

"You'll not die today. Or tomorrow. You're talking about dying again when I want to talk about living."

"But it has to mean something. The fact that You're here with me, right?"

"It does mean something. But not what you think."

"It's OK, I don't mind dying. If it means I can be with You." Maybe it wasn't a near-death experience, maybe she had died. "I can't believe You're here. I don't deserve this."

"Love isn't deserved. It just is."

Tears slid down her cheeks. "But I haven't been very good . . . not much of a Christian. Too worried about . . . about other things."

"Still, I am with you always. Even when you're too busy to notice . . . or to care."

She fell to her knees. "I . . . you . . ." She couldn't find the words. "Love."

His hands moved to both sides of her cheeks. "I feel your love, your faith, your loyalty. You are my faithful servant, my sweet Rachel."

"I haven't been all that faithful."

"I know, but still I love you."

"In fact, most of the time I haven't even thought about You. Sure we go to church, but I've been too busy worrying about my life. And what I want. It's always about me, me, me."

He reached out and took her hand. His other hand still touched her cheek. She lost track of time as they stayed in that position. Her heart swelled so much that love didn't seem to be the right word. She'd never experienced such . . . such love and acceptance.

So much was communicated in that span of time. Rachel had no sense of how long they stood that way. As Jesus took His hand from her cheek, she glanced at her broken body.

A man in a white coat touch his beard and then said, "She's stabilized. Let's get her in for an MRI. Stat."

The gurney her body was on moved out of the room.

"Ready to take that walk?"

They moved from the emergency room with no effort on her part.

The man from the emergency room

walked up to her boss, Dan.

A moment later Cooper rushed over to Dan. Her boss put an arm around her husband and spoke soft words. Cooper collapsed into Dan's arms.

"Are you sure I didn't die?" Rachel asked. "Cooper looks very upset."

"Of course he loves you very much, but no you didn't die.."

"I suppose You would know. I can't believe You're actually here with me." She smiled. "Don't say it. I remember. You are with me always, right?"

"Right. It seems as if people forget that so often."

Reverend Smith, the preacher who would lead the conference she was organizing in three days, came into the waiting room.

Jesus pointed at the men, now holding hands and praying. "They are good and faithful servants."

"I know. I'm so blessed to have a godly husband in my life."

"So you are." He looped his arm through hers. "Now it's time to have a serious discussion."

"About what?"

"About living, not dying. About your future."

"I don't know. It didn't look as if I have

much of a future from where I'm standing."

"Be not troubled. You have a long future ahead of you, my dear Rachel."

"Really?"

"Really. The question is what do you want to do with that future? You can continue on the way you have been or you can choose something else. You can choose a different life. One that will make a difference."

"Something else? But I wouldn't even have an idea of what else I could do."

"God created you, each of you, for a purpose. His purpose is your dream. Are you living that dream right now, my dear sweet Rachel?"

"Well, I wouldn't exactly say that." Of course, it hadn't been her dream to work seventy hours a week. Too busy to spend time with her husband. Too busy to have a family. Too busy to . . .

"Then what is your dream?"

"I don't know. I guess when I was younger my dream was to help people. Sick people. But then I grew up. I didn't have enough money or enough brains to become a doctor, so I didn't." She shrugged. "It even says somewhere in the Bible that you need to put away childish things when you become an adult."

"There is nothing childish about dreams,

my dear Rachel. God gives you those dreams. His purpose is your dream. I need an answer from you."

"What's the question? I didn't hear a question."

"Are you ready to follow your dreams?

"I guess so. Is that what you want me to do?"

"The choice is yours. So here's the real question I need answered. Do you want to be healed or to be a healer?"

She stared at him. "I don't think I understand the question."

"It's a simple question, my sweet Rachel."

"Well, if I say I want to be a healer, I won't be healed, and then I'll die. And that means I won't be around to be a healer. Yet if I say I want to be healed, then I'm being selfish and that's a sin."

"I can see why you're confused. I'm not trying to trick you. I'm simply giving you a choice."

"Good. I thought maybe it was the head injury I must have."

"Your answer has nothing to do with whether you die today or not. You will not die today or any day from the injuries you sustained in this accident. Or from any accident you may have in the future, so you can stop worrying about trucks, especially when you pass them."

"Oh." That was a secret phobia of hers. "I guess I don't really have any secrets from You."

"No you don't. You'll be fine."

"Oh. In that case, what was the question again?" She laughed. "I'm kidding. I remember the question."

"That's one of the things I love most about you. A great sense of humor."

"It seems to get me in trouble sometimes."

"The same thing happened to Me when I was on earth. I remember this one time . . ." He smiled. "Well, we don't have time to reminisce right now."

She squeezed his hand. "Oh, I would love nothing more than to do that. Right now and forever. I want to hear about your childhood. And what kind of a man Joseph was and what happened to him. And did you ever fall in love? And . . ."

"And someday, we'll be able to talk about all those things and more. But not today. The question remains."

"Right? Do I want to be healed or be a healer?"

"That's the question."

"I know what my answer is, but I don't quite understand how . . ."

"Life here on earth is not about certainty,

my dear child. Life here is about faith, hope, and love. And love being the greatest."

She nudged him, her shoulder touching his. "Could we spend more time discussing all the things You love about me?"

He smiled. "I will love you always. There is nothing you can do to make Me love you less. Love simply is."

Tears streamed down her cheeks. "That is so . . . amazing. So wonderful."

"Be sure to remember that, later."

"I don't quite see how I could ever forget. Or even one word of what we've talked about. I suppose You're waiting for my answer. But of course You know it already, don't you?"

He nodded. "But I want you to say it aloud. It has to be your choice. Not mine."

"I want to be a healer. I even started out in premed, but changed my mind. It would have taken too long."

"You are an impatient one. Are you sure about this?"

She wasn't sure about anything at all. "I want to be a healer."

"It won't be an easy journey. But this I tell you, you have all that you need to be successful in that journey. If it's what you choose."

"I do choose it. I want to be a healer."

His arms went around her. "Then so you shall be, my child."

When he stepped away, they were in a new room.

An MRI machine enclosed her still body.

"It is time for Me to go. Remember all that I've told you today. And remember I am with you . . ." His hand slipped from hers.

She finished his statement. "Always."

He smiled and nodded. "Always."

She floated downward. Rachel opened her eyes, knowing exactly where she was and why. None of it mattered. Not slamming head long into a truck. Not whatever was wrong with her. She'd seen Jesus. Met Him. Talked to Him. He'd told her that He loved her, held her hand, and even hugged her. And given her the gift to heal people. Joy filled her heart.

Cooper sat beside the bed, his hand in hers.

She squeezed it as she opened her eyes. "Jesus was here."

"Oh, thank You, God. You're awake." He touched her cheek. "I was so worried . . . no, not worried. Terrified. You're my life."

"And you're mine." A love that couldn't be expressed in words filled her heart, her soul, for her husband. She repeated the words from before. "Jesus was here. With me."

"I know. I felt His presence too. I've been praying continuously. And not just me." Her husband's hand squeezed hers. "A worldwide prayer alert was sent out on your behalf from —"

"Reverend Smith."

His eyes widened. "How did you know that? He had his congregation across the world praying for you." Tears streamed down her big, tough husband's face. "I'm so glad God brought you back to me."

"Jesus was here. With me. He held my hand. Touched my cheek. We talked."

Cooper's blue eyes widened, but he nodded with a smile. "With Jesus? I think I'm a little jealous."

Just like her sweet husband not to question her sanity, but simply to believe her. "Don't be. He had nice things to say about you."

"Right?"

"I'm serious."

He pushed the button in his hand. "I'm sure you are."

"Why'd you press that? To tell them I lost my mind?"

"Not at all. They told me to do that the moment you woke up."

48

A nurse rushed in. "Is she awake?"

He nodded, and then turned to Rachel. "And talking. She seems fine."

"Good to see you finally decided to join us. We were getting a bit concerned that you didn't want to wake up." The nurse nodded.

"How long have I been unconscious?"

"A while."

Before she could ask how long a while was, another doctor walked in. "Nice to meet you, Mrs. Summers. I'm Dr. Wyatt."

"What happened to the other doctor?"

"Other doctor?

"Yeah, the young one with a beard."

"That's Dr. Seaton. But there's no way you could know that. You were completely unconscious when you were brought in."

"And yet I saw him stick a tube of some sort down my throat."

He looked at her, and then shrugged. "He's in emergency, you're in the ICU now. But not for long now that you're awake."

"So how badly did I get hurt?" She braced for bad news.

"It's an amazing thing." The doctor shook his head. "You don't have any serious injuries from the accident. Some cuts and lacerations but not a broken bone or even a fractured one. Nothing."

Jesus had been right.

"Why was she unconscious for so long?" Cooper asked.

"Sometimes the body does what the body needs. We don't always have explanations."

Rachel knew it was so she could visit with Jesus. "How long was I unconscious?"

The doctor checked the tablet computer he held. "Five days."

"Are you kidding me? That means I missed —"

"Don't worry about the conference. From what I hear, it went perfectly." Cooper held her hand. "Dan said you were so perfectly organized, all they had to do was read your to-do list. Everything got done. And the conference went without a hitch."

"I thought I was here maybe an hour or two. No wonder you were worried. But if nothing's wrong with me, I can go home now, right?"

Cooper laughed. "I told the doctor once you woke up he wouldn't be able to keep you in that bed."

"That's exactly where she's staying." The doctor held up a hand. "For now. As long as everything goes fine, you can go home tomorrow. No need to rush things. After all, you were hit by a truck."

"But she's OK?" Cooper asked.

"Fit as a fiddle from what I can see. I don't have a clue how that happened. She's a walking miracle."

A miracle. That was exactly right. Her eyes filled with tears as she thought back to the conversation with Jesus. She couldn't wait to tell Cooper all about it. And that Jesus had given her the gift of healing. She focused back on the doctor.

"We found something else." His tone was serious.

Cooper's hand squeezed hers. "Something else? You never said anything to me about something else being wrong."

"I wanted to wait until she was awake. One step at a time. When we did the —"

"MRI?" she asked.

The doctor looked surprised. "How did you know we did one? You weren't conscious at the time."

"I saw it."

"Saw it?" His voice was skeptical.

She nodded. "Just before Jesus left, he walked me into the MRI room. Then he let go of my hand and I floated back into my body."

He stared at her. "Just before Jesus left?"

"Yes, Jesus was here. With me. He held my hand and we walked and talked."

The doctor smiled. "I'm a believer."

51

"It was amazing."

"I'm sure it was. You aren't the first of my patients to tell me about a near-death experience, but you're the first to offer a shred of evidence. There's no way you could know about the MRI or Dr. Seaton. That was done when you first got here. And you were very unconscious at the time. Can you tell me anything else about your experience?"

"The MRI technician was a man . . . with red hair."

"Wow. That's amazing, you're right. I want to hear more about this later, but right now I have to tell you something the MRI found."

"What?"

"There's no easy way to say this. You have bilateral brain tumors."

Her heart fluttered. "Brain tumors."

To be healed or be a healer?

Now she understood what Jesus meant.

"They're almost always benign. But they still have to be treated." The doctor put a hand on her shoulder. "Don't panic. They're serious but manageable. They're called schwannomas and are usually part of a genetic condition called Neurofibromatosis, Type Two."

To be healed or to be a healer?

"I don't understand."

"Your nerves are surrounded by something called the myelin sheath. The myelin sheath is made up of Schwann cells. The tumors are formed from them. Thus, they're called schwannomas."

She was still shocked by the diagnosis. "I can't believe I have brain tumors. I haven't had any headaches or anything."

"No dizziness. Maybe some hearing loss?"

"No. Oh, wait, that's not true. I did have some dizziness awhile back. I just thought it was from the stress of moving and starting a new job. It went away so I didn't worry about it."

"It was more than stress. I'll set you up with a neurologist, an expert in the field."

She scooted to a sitting position. "I want to know more about these tumors and the neurofib . . . what did you call it again?"

"Neurofibromatosis Type Two. I thought you might." He handed her some papers. "Here's some more information about them and about NF2." He left the room.

Cooper's brows were furrowed as he read the papers the doctor had given them.

She touched his arm. "Forget about that for now. I need to tell you about Jesus."

He looked up but his expression still screamed 'worried'.

"He gave me the gift of healing."

No longer slouching or looking at the puzzle, Nia's dark brown eyes glittered. With hope? Or was it something else? "Now, I get it. Auntie brought me here so you could heal me. Whattaya gonna do? Put your hand on my forehead, knock me down, and tell me I'm healed." She stood up but still leaned on the card table for support. "I can't believe this. You're a scammer. Gonna take all my auntie's money by telling her you'll heal me. And when the money's gone, I'll still be on my way to dead."

"That's not why you're here, Nia."

"You're right." She swept her hand over the puzzle pieces as they scattered on the floor. "That won't happen. I'm outta here. I'm not staying here one minute longer. I'll not let you steal Auntie's money. She works hard for it. She's spent more than enough on me, as it is. No more. I won't let this happen." She looked around as if trying to figure out a means of escape. "I'll walk all the way back to Atlanta if I have to."

"I'm not stealing anything, Nia." Rachel knelt, picked up puzzle pieces, and put them back on the table. "I don't take money."

Nia glared at Rachel. "You expect me to believe that? No wonder you been acting all nice and friendly to me. Telling me how special I am. You just want my auntie's money."

"You are special. To me and to God."

"Yeah, whatevs."

"I don't take money for you to come here. That's not how it works."

"Then why you being so nice to me? Why are you even letting me be here if Auntie didn't pay you? It has to cost something. You don't get nothing for free in this world. I know that even if I'm a kid."

"Because I love you."

"You don't love me. You don't even know me."

"I do love you, because of who you are."

"And just exactly who am I? What makes me so special?"

"You're a child of God. And if God loves you, which He does, then I love you. It's that simple."

Nia stared at Rachel, a young, frightened girl who was struggling with big issues. Tears welled in her eyes. "I want to go home."

"And you will, but not yet. Your aunt will pick you up next week as she promised. You're here for help. We should get along, don't you think?"

"I want to go now. Where's a phone?

Auntie wouldn't let me bring my cell phone. She needs to come and get me. I'm not staying in this crazy place with a crazy white lady." Nia glared.

Rachel smiled. "Aren't you going to add, 'no offense'?"

"No. I meant to offend."

"Well, none taken. You aren't happy right now, but I promise this is not a scam and you will feel better soon."

"Why?"

"Because we're working on the puzzle together."

Nia struggled to her feet. "I ain't working on nothing. Just cause I can't leave doesn't mean I have to listen to you. I'm going to my room."

"Nia, please . . ." Her voice trailed off.

Nia marched out of the room. A moment later the stair lift came to life.

3

Nia stepped off the lift and stared at the doors. Which one was her room? She didn't know. She sat down, and gave in to the tears that had threatened since Auntie had deserted her. Nia had always found a way to get what she wanted, especially since she'd gotten sick. But not this time. She'd thrown tantrum after tantrum.

Auntie remained firm.

Nia was spending the week at this stupid place. And now she knew why. Because some crazy faith healer had convinced Auntie that she could keep her from dying. And no matter what the lady said, Nia knew her aunt had probably spent a lot of money. What a waste.

"What are you doing?"

She startled at the voice but kept her face hidden. "Nothing. Go away."

Brandon sat down beside her. "Having a pity party, huh?"

"I said go away."

"I'm guessing you don't know which room is yours."

She looked up.

With his curly brown hair and those bright blue eyes, Brandon was cute. But that probably just meant he was conceited.

"I said leave me alone."

"I can show you which one is yours. Since I'm the one who brought your stuff up. Unless you like having your pity party out here in the hall so everyone can see."

"Not having a pity party."

He grinned. "Looks kind of like you are."

"Go away."

"OK. Your wish is my command." He stood and turned to leave.

"After you show me which room is mine."

"Not a problem." He held out a hand.

She stared.

"I'm not gonna bite."

"Fine." She held out her hand.

He helped her up.

Nia wanted to push him away. She didn't want to be nice to anybody at this crazy place. But Auntie's manners were too ingrained in her. "Thanks."

He pointed, and then opened a door. "This is your room." He opened the door.

She walked in.

"So what's your problem?" he asked.

None of your business. "I have cancer — leukemia. And the doctors said I'm not responding to the treatment so there's nothing they can do to help me. Just a matter of time before I die."

Instead of looking shocked or sad, he just nodded. "That's not what I was asking. I meant what's your problem with being here at Puzzle House? It's a good place. You're blessed to be here."

"Don't tell me you believe in all this healing stuff?"

"I believe in God so, yes, I believe God heals."

"What would you know about it? You look strong and healthy to me."

"I know what I know."

"Whatevs." She rolled her eyes for emphasis.

"Well, I'll leave you to your pity party since you're determined to be miserable. Rachel's a nice lady so you should give her a chance." He left.

Not much sympathy from him considering she was the one dying. What did he know about anything, anyway? He should be a little nicer.

Nia closed the door and flopped down on the bed. Why was Auntie doing this to her?

59

Everyone knew she would die from this stupid disease. Yet Auntie kept saying Nia would be fine. She'd beat this and get healthy and have a wonderful life. Yeah, right!

After the doctors had said there'd be no more treatments, Nia had stopped letting her friends come to visit. Most days she just watched TV and cried. She tried not to cry when Auntie was around because it made Auntie cry, too.

Their house was sad these days.

And then Auntie started talking on the phone, but she kept leaving the room so Nia couldn't hear. Auntie started smiling as if she had a secret.

Nia asked what was going on.

"I have a surprise for you." That's what Auntie had said.

Yeah, some surprise. Bringing her to the middle of nowhere and making her stay for the week. Without TV or a phone. With a crazy white lady who thought she was a healer. Well, Nia knew how this would end.

Even if nobody else did.

Patience — one of the many things Rachel wasn't very good at. She sat on the porch, praying for enough patience and wisdom to help Nia. She focused in on God's beauty

60

surrounding her.

The fall colors were at their height. Another week or so and they'd be gone, but for now they were perfect. From where she sat, if she leaned out just a bit she could see the pond shimmering from the afternoon sun.

Her gaze drank in the beauty even as her soul drank in the peace. She had a feeling she might need an extra dose of that. Unlike most of the guests at Puzzle House, Nia didn't want to be here. That made things a bit more difficult.

Every guest at Puzzle House had one thing in common. They needed something. All thought they came for one reason, but many found something much different than what they'd been searching for. God seemed to always work it out for the best.

Rachel checked the long braid that fell down her back, now sprinkled with gray. Long ago, she'd given up fashion for comfort. Today she wore a long, blue skirt with tiny purple flowers. The simple top she wore matched the flowers. And she had slipped her feet into sandals this morning. She probably looked like an aging hippie.

Not that Nia would even know the term.

Rachel's feet pushed against the slats of knotty pine wood. The squeak made a rhythmic sound with each rock. There was no rush.

Nia would be here for a week or even more. And if she remained uncooperative, then that would be up to God to change Nia's heart. The poor girl had been through so much in her young years. It wasn't any surprise that she was angry and fearful. *Please, God, give her the courage to open up to me. And more important, to open up to You.*

The door opened.

"Annie."

"Rachel, don't get up. I am more than capable of guiding this thing to where I want to go."

"I know that. I just thought to help, if needed."

"That's the problem. You help too much."

"I do no such thing. I sit around, read the Bible, and pray. And talk with nice people like you."

"And deal with angry teenagers." Annie locked the brakes on the wheelchair. "That Nia seems to be quite the handful."

"It hasn't been easy for her."

"So I heard when I was in The Meeting Room. I wasn't trying to eavesdrop."

"That's OK. Puzzle House isn't about secrets."

"True, but it seems as if we all have a few

anyway. Just wanted to let you know I'll be leaving tonight. My daughter will be picking me up after dinner."

"Do you think things will be all right with the two of you, now?"

"I hope so. She'll not be happy when I tell her I'm moving into an assisted living facility. But it's what I want. It's for the best. For everyone."

"I think it'll be all about how you present it to her. If she thinks you're doing it to make it easier on her, then that'll make her feel guilty. And then you'll have another fight about it."

Annie gave a warm smile. "I think you're right. But I miss being around people and that's why I want to go to the facility. I think she'll understand I don't like being alone anymore in my condition. I know it's best for me and really, best for her, too. She'll know I'm always safe and she can visit anytime."

"That sounds like a good plan, Annie."

"I really appreciate the time I've had here. It's been . . . good. And helpful. I'm ready to face this next phase of my life."

"That doesn't surprise me. You've always done that."

"Just tried to do the best with what God gave me."

"Amen to that! Still you've had an amazing life and still have more to do with it."

"I just did what I had to do."

Rachel just smiled. Annie still had a lot more living to do. "Could you do me a favor?"

"If I can, I'll be glad to do it."

"Can you pray for Nia this week? And keep on praying for her."

"Now that's something I can still do."

The door opened.

Nia's eyes were puffy. She looked at the two women and chose a rocking chair on the other side of the porch away from them.

Annie smiled at Rachel, and then maneuvered her chair closer to the girl. "Nia, why don't you come sit with us? We're not doing anything important. Just sitting and chatting."

Nia said nothing.

"I'd really like to get to know you a little before I leave this evening," Annie said.

"What's to know?" Nia muttered. "I'm fifteen and dying."

"Oh, I want to know all about you. What you like to do for fun? Do you have a boyfriend? What's your favorite class in school?"

"Yea, like any boy would want to have a girlfriend who's about to kick the bucket?"

She touched her head. "Boys don't like bald."

Annie motioned. "Well come over and talk with us anyway."

Nia heaved a large sigh but moved to a closer chair, still not looking at Rachel.

Rachel put her hand out and smiled. "Friends?"

A little smile graced Nia's face. "I guess."

"Can we shake on it?" Rachel pressed her hand, hoping all the warmth and love was transferred to Nia. "I'm so glad. It would be a long week for both of us if not."

"I 'spose so." Nia shrugged. "So you got more of the story to tell me?"

"I'll tell you more tomorrow when we're working on your puzzle. Right now, I want you to meet Annie. She doesn't look it but she's ninety-five."

"Don't listen to her. I look every bit of my ninety-five years." Annie winked at her. "And that's all right. I've earned every one of my wrinkles."

"What's it like being that old?"

"Well, there are good things and bad. The bad is I have another ache some place new every day. But the good is that I know these aches aren't going to last forever."

Nia started to say something but stopped.

Annie laughed. "Yes, dear. I mean exactly

what you're thinking. I'm going to die one of these days. Not sure when God'll call me home. But when he does all the pains and tears will be gone. And I'll get to live in glory with Him forever. Amen."

Rachel chimed in. "Amen."

"It sounds like you don't care if you die."

"I wouldn't exactly say that, but I'm ready when God's ready." She smiled at Nia. Her voice was filled with compassion.

"Annie's lived an amazing life. Her husband died in World War II. She had five kids to take care of. And she did more than take care of them. She became a teacher, and then kept on going to school and got a PhD in education. She's met three presidents while working on education policies for this country."

"Three presidents? That's cool."

"But that's enough about me. I've lived my years. I can sure understand why you're angry about being sick."

Nia didn't say anything.

"And you know what? God understands, too. You really need to tell Him all about it. I think you need a good yelling session with Him. Go ahead. He's strong enough to handle it."

"He's already mad at me. I don't want to make him madder." Her voice was barely a whisper.

"Nah, He won't get mad at you, sweetie. He loves you." Annie said. "Go ahead."

Nia shook her head.

"OK, I'll go first." Annie looked upwards and yelled. "Hey, God. I'm really mad that I can't walk anymore. Do you hear me? I want to walk again."

"My turn." Rachel said, not as loudly as Annie, but loud enough. "And God, I'm really mad that Nia's feeling so tired and weak."

"Me, too." Nia added.

"Your turn, sweetie. Give him what-for," Annie giggled.

"It's not fair, God. Why do I have to be sick? Why do I have to die?" Tears streamed down Nia's face. "I don't want to die, God. I really don't."

Rachel moved from her seat to her knees, grabbing hold of Nia's hand. Annie picked up the other. Quietly Rachel said, "Tell him what you feel. And loudly."

"It's not fair. It's not fair." Nia kept saying the phrase over and over, until she was overcome with tears. Heart-wrenching sobs emanated for a few moments, and then ceased.

Annie patted her hand. "Alrighty, then. Do you feel better?"

Nia wiped her face, giving them a watery smile. "I think I do. But I'm sort of afraid."

"Of what?"

"That I might get hit by lightning."

"Don't worry about that. It's not the first time I yelled at God. And he never did strike me with lightning."

Nia giggled. "That's good to hear."

The door opened.

"What's all the noise?" Brandon asked.

"Girl talk," Rachel responded.

"In other words, none of my business?"

"Something like that." Rachel grinned. "But that doesn't mean we don't love you too."

"Good to know." He jangled the keys in his hand. "I'm going to town to get that order you put in at the store. Need anything else while I'm there?"

"Not me, but I'm guessing Nia might enjoy the drive."

He looked at her. "Wanna go?"

Nia shrugged. "I guess. It's not like I got anything else to do."

"Great but I have to warn you about something." He looped his arm through hers. "No pity parties allowed in my car."

She pulled away.

"Come on." He snagged her arm again. "I was just kidding. I really would like some company."

"So how long have you been coming to Puzzle House?" Nia asked as they drove along the rural road.

"This is my fifth year. I come every year for a few weeks in the summer."

"Don't you get bored? There's nothing to do."

"Nothing to do? Are you kidding me? There's horses and the other animals. And fishing. And swimming."

"Like I said, nothing to do."

"OK, city girl. What kind of things do you do in the big city?"

"Well, not a whole lot these days."

He wiggled a finger at her. "No pity parties allowed. Remember, city girl?"

She laughed. "Fine, country boy. Let's see. I like to go to the mall with my friends."

"Of course."

"Sometimes we go to concerts. Free ones and sometimes Auntie even gives me money for a real concert."

"The mall and concerts." He made a face. "So far I'm not hearing anything I like. Now if it were up to me I'd go to every museum in the city."

"Museums? Why?"

"Why? Are you kidding me? There's so

much amazing art out there."

"If you say so." She sighed theatrically. "I have something else I like to do but . . ."

"But what?"

"It's sort of a secret."

Still holding the wheel with one hand, he rubbed both hands together. "I love secrets."

"Keep your hands on the wheel, country boy."

"So what's the secret? I bet it's a good one."

She laughed. "Not really. I —"

"Wait. Wait. Let me guess."

"You'll never guess, but go ahead."

"Don't call me a goat head."

"I didn't." She laughed. "Oh. I just got it. Go Ahead. Goat Head. I guess that's country boy humor."

"It made you laugh. Let's see. How about the zoo?"

"No."

"It's museums, right? You're an art lover just like me."

"Boring."

"Churches. You go around the city and visit all the beautiful churches."

"No, but that's a good idea."

"Mmm . . . let me think. Can I see your hand?" He ran his index finger down her palm.

70

She didn't move or breathe.

"You have long graceful fingers. Beautiful, in fact. I'll take a guess and say . . . music. You either play the piano or the guitar."

"I can't believe you figured it out."

"The fingers. Dead giveaway. They were made to make music."

"I don't know about all that."

"So which is it? The piano or the guitar?"

"Both, actually." She took her hand back.

"What kind of music?"

"All kinds actually. Before I got too sick I was listening and trying to play some of the classical music. But I'm not very good at it."

"I'll be the judge of that."

"Don't see how that'll happen. Since I don't play anymore."

"No pity parties, city girl."

She tossed her head. "It's not a pity party, just a statement of fact."

"I don't know. It sounded awfully close to a pity party."

"You know you really could have a little more sympathy for the sick girl."

"No way. You can get that from everyone else. Not me. I don't have time for pity parties. And they don't help anyway. Believe me, I know."

"How do you know that?"

71

He pulled into a grocery store and put the car in park. His soft blue eyes were filled with sadness, but then he smiled. "Do you think you're the only one who has problems?" He opened his door.

"Hold on, country boy. What are you saying? That you're sick too?"

He shrugged. "I'm saying everyone has problems. We can let them dictate how we live or we can keep our eyes on Jesus. Now, let's go. We've got things to do and people to see."

He slammed the door shut before she ask another question. A moment later he opened her door. Wow. No one had ever done that for her before. He held out a hand and smiled.

Nia put her hand in his and grinned.

4

The next morning Nia walked in just as the bread popped up from the toaster. Rachel placed the toast on a plate and put it in front of her. "Want some eggs to go with it?"

"No, I don't eat much in the morning. It makes me kind of sick."

She did look sick, her eyes were dull and her face pale. Rachel's heart went out to her.

Nia picked up a glass of orange juice. "Is this for me?"

"Sure."

After taking a drink, she smiled. "Wow. That's the best orange juice I ever had."

"It's fresh-squeezed."

"Where's everyone else?"

"Well Annie left last night after you went up to bed. And Brandon's around somewhere. Not quite sure what he's up to today. So it's just the two of us. Which is good. I wanted to spend some time helping you with your puzzle."

"Do you mean my puzzle for real, or my life puzzle?"

Rachel smiled. "Maybe a little of both."

After eating they walked to the puzzle room together.

Rachel used her cane.

"Why do you need that?"

"The brain tumors messed up my hearing and my balance."

"If you're a healer, you should be able to heal yourself. Right?"

"I wish, but it didn't work out that way. Do you remember what Jesus asked me?"

"Not really. By then I was getting mad at you. I wasn't really listening."

"He gave me a choice. To be healed or to be a healer? I made the choice to be a healer which apparently meant that I had to live with the consequences of my brain tumors."

I think you shoulda picked to be healed."

"At the time I didn't even know I had brain tumors. And even when I learned about them, I didn't think it was that big of a deal. At first."

"So was that true? They wasn't no big deal."

"Oh no, I was very, very wrong about that. They were a big deal." She raised her arms separating them as far as they could go, her cane waving in the air. "Huge deal. They completely changed my life. And not necessarily in a good way. It's been a long time but I still struggle with the aftereffects of them."

"Like not walking real good?"

"Among other things."

"But they were benign. So how bad could they be? It's not like you had cancer like me."

"That's very true and I wouldn't ever say what I had was as bad as cancer. But really, when it comes to being ill or sick or having a condition, it's not fair to compare one to the other. When you don't feel good, you don't feel good."

"I suppose that's true." It made her think of Brandon the country boy. What was his problem? He looked healthy enough so it must be something else. Probably family problems. She thought of asking Rachel but had a feeling the woman wouldn't tell her.

"Can you keep a secret?" Rachel whispered, as she looked around.

"Sure."

"I really learned to hate that word. Benign. Everyone kept telling me. Aren't you lucky that they're benign? I'd smile and agree, but inside I wanted to scream at them. Look

75

at me. Look at my problems. Look at what I can't do anymore. I knew they meant well, but it was a bit of an irritation at the time. And yet I knew they were right. It could have been lots worse, but still, it made me sort of mad."

"Yea, a lot worse. So what else did the tumors do to you?" She touched Rachel's cane.

Rachel lifted up her hair to reveal a hearing aid. "I lost all my hearing in one ear and some in the other. That's why if I say something that doesn't make sense, it's probably because I heard it wrong."

"Oh, I thought it was because you're a crazy white lady." Nia grinned. "No offense."

Rachel chuckled. "None taken."

"So I guess Jesus meant it when He told you to pick one or the other, huh? You'd think He'd want you to be really healthy so you could go around healing everyone."

"I would have liked that to happen, but there were things I needed to learn. And I probably wouldn't have learned them if I'd stayed healthy."

"What kinds of things?"

"Compassion. Understanding what it really means to someone when they're very sick. How it affects every part of their life."

Rachel sat down at Nia's puzzle table. "Want to hear a little more about it?"

Nia nodded as she sat down.

"Like you, I thought to myself, Jesus made me a healer so I should be able to heal myself. But that's not how it happened."

There was nothing in the rule book that said she couldn't heal herself. Not that she'd found the rule book yet, but she knew she'd figure it out. Sooner or later. After all Jesus had promised her she would be a healer. That was the only thing she was sure of.

There wasn't a whole lot of information available about neurofibromatosis. What she could find didn't sound good. But the doctor's visit the day before hadn't been all gloom and doom. He'd been quite hopeful. In the grand scheme of things, the NF2 hadn't sounded all that bad. Still after all she'd read the past few days, she wanted to go curl up and cry. A lot.

Cooper would tell her to stop focusing on the negative and look on the bright side.

Thanks to the accident, they'd found the tumors early. Hopefully, that meant they wouldn't cause all the problems she'd been reading about.

Of course, Cooper wasn't the one with tumors in his head.

She was scheduled for her first treatment in two weeks. They called it Gamma Knife surgery — it didn't involve a knife or surgery at all, but was a type of radiation treatment.

She'd wanted them to do both sides at once, but apparently that was a big no-no.

"Not happening." The doctor had said. He'd refused to even discuss the possibility. One treatment now, then in a year they'd talk about the second treatment. That seemed overcautious, but he was the doctor.

Still she wanted to get it over with so she could get back to her life. And to healing other people.

The doorbell rang.

"I'll get it, hon. It's probably Dan," she called out to Cooper in his own office upstairs.

Her boss had called and asked to stop by. Besides checking on her, he was probably worried about how her health would impact her job.

She would have been in his place.

"OK." Cooper's disembodied voice floated down.

Rachel opened the door.

Dan stood in front of a backdrop of sunshine, the first they'd had in weeks.

Winter was gloomy in Ohio. It was hard to get used to.

Seeing the light reminded her of Jesus. Suddenly she was overwhelmed by the whole hospital experience once again. Her cheek tingled where Jesus had held her face in his hands. Tears filled her eyes.

"Everything OK?" Dan's voice brought her back to earth.

"Oh, yeah. Sorry. The sun blinded me."

"Yeah, not something we're used to seeing at this time of the year."

"I don't know how you people stand it. Come on in."

"You people? Well, you're one of us now. So you'll learn to live with it too. How are you feeling?" He unbuttoned his coat.

She took the coat. "Are you being polite or do you want to know the truth?"

"The truth. That's why I'm here."

She hadn't decided just how much she would tell him. There was no way of knowing his religious beliefs. Religion had no place in the workplace these days. "Let me hang this up, then I'll get us some coffee."

Cooper bounded down the steps. "I'll get the coffee, hon. You sit down and rest."

She smiled at Dan. "He's been like this since I got home from the hospital. I think he's more worried about my tumors than I am."

"That's not surprising. I'd be the same way with Claudia. Plus you did get hit by a truck. I can't believe you weren't seriously hurt."

"It was definitely a miracle." She motioned him toward the living room.

They sat down.

"Well, I'm not sure how I am. Still a little shocked by the whole thing. I don't feel as if there's anything wrong with me."

"Well, that's good."

"I guess but it sort of makes it seem not quite real. I'll have my first treatment in a few weeks and we'll go from there. In the meantime, I plan to come back to work until then, take a few days off after the treatment and then back to work the following Monday."

"Are you sure about that?"

"I don't see why not. The doctor said there wouldn't be any reason why I couldn't. But there's something else I want to talk to you about."

He nodded.

"I saw Jesus when I was in the coma. He talked with me. He touched me."

"Jesus?" His eyes widened and his voice filled with skepticism. "It was probably a dream, Rachel. I don't really put much stock in those near-death experiences."

"I never did either. Until now." She'd suspected this might be his reaction. "But you do believe they're possible, right?"

"Lots of people have had them, I guess. But then again I've never had one so what do I know. I've even read some scientific explanations for them. Something to do with some chemicals in the brain."

Seeing Jesus hadn't happened because of some chemical in her brain. It had been real. She leaned forward. "Not only did I talk with Jesus, but he gave me a gift while I was in my coma."

"I didn't hear anybody call it a coma, they said you were unconscious."

"OK, unconscious. Anyway, Jesus and I took a walk while I wasn't awake. Whatever you want to call it. And when I woke up, I knew things I had no way of knowing."

"Like what?" A spark of interest was in Dan's eyes.

"I knew what the one doctor looked like who worked on me in the emergency room. And that I'd had an MRI and what color the technician's hair was."

"Interesting. I still can't say I really believe it."

"What's interesting?" Cooper asked as he

walked in with a tray of cookies and mugs. He set the tray on the coffee table then sat beside Rachel.

"She was telling me about how she knew things when she woke up. And her visit with Jesus."

"Unbelievable, huh?"

"Don't tell me you believe it, Cooper?"

"Of course, I do. We've talked about it several times. I never get tired of hearing about it. I'm a little jealous."

"You really believe her? That she talked with Jesus?"

"Don't you?"

Dan leaned forward and picked up a chocolate chip cookie, avoiding her gaze. Clearly he was uncomfortable with the topic. "I'm sure she dreamt it. But that's about as far as I'll go. Real or not real. I have no way of knowing that."

"I can understand that but it's really a matter of faith. God is a supernatural God. That means he can do supernatural things. Even when we don't understand them." Cooper smiled.

"You make the best cookies, Cooper." Dan took a bite with a look towards Rachel. "You're a lucky woman."

"More than you know. That's just the tip of the iceberg. He's a great cook. And he

82

loves doing it. He's such a blessing from God. And I tell him and everyone who'll listen to me every chance I get."

"That's nice."

"Also, when you have a visit from Jesus it changes everything. Everything includes my job."

"Are you saying that you're quitting?"

"Not at all, but I wanted you to be aware that I'm a different person now than I was a few weeks ago."

"You look the same to me."

"Jesus told me I could be healed or be a healer. At the time I had no idea what he meant because he assured me that I wouldn't have any long-term injuries from the accident. Of course now, I know he was talking about the tumors."

"You really believe if you'd chosen to be healed, you'd be all right now?"

"Absolutely. Without a doubt."

"Then you must really regret your decision, huh?"

"Not at all. I always wanted to help sick people. I don't regret my decision. I'd do it again if given the choice. I'm not quite sure how it'll affect me yet. I just wanted to share my experience with you."

"I'm not sure what you want me to say, Rachel. Are you sure you're not resigning your position? I don't see how you'll have the time to heal people and do your job."

"I don't know how either. But God will work it out. And I have no plans to quit at this point. I just thought you should know I'm not the same person I was before."

"Well, you'll be fine after your treatment. Take all the time you need to recuperate. Your job will be waiting. You did a great job with the conference, by the way. Reverend Smith was impressed. He said he couldn't wait until next year's conference."

"I'm not worried about my job. I just needed you to be aware that . . ." She stopped. "I just needed you to understand that I saw Jesus. Talked with Him. And that it was utterly amazing."

He shrugged. "Well, it's not every day someone has a sit-down with the Big Guy."

"Actually we didn't sit at all. We walked, well, more like floated around the hospital. Do you want to hear about it?"

"I'm sure it was wonderful and as long as it doesn't affect your job, it doesn't matter to me." After a few more pleasantries, he left.

"I thought he'd be more impressed." Rachel was disappointed.

"Well, not everyone has the same beliefs we do."

"Still when someone tells you they spent time with Jesus, you'd think they'd want to hear about it. No matter what your beliefs are."

"I'd think so. But that's just me."

"He didn't stay around long enough for me to tell him that I wrote a magazine article about my experience."

"Did you decide on a title yet?"

"I was thinking 'A Visit With Jesus', but I'm not sure. If this column goes long-term, I can't just talk about that one experience forever. Can I?"

"Probably not."

"Any ideas?"

" 'The Healing Journey', then you can talk about your own medical condition. Or maybe 'Journey with Jesus'? That gives you a lot of options."

"Ooh, I like that. 'Journey with Jesus' has a nice ring to it."

"And then, of course, your first column could be 'A Visit With Jesus'. I think you should lay it out right from the start. So readers know where you're coming from.

"Sounds like a plan to me." She picked up a cookie. "I really wish I'd remembered to tell Dan about the magazine, but I guess it doesn't matter. There's no reason it should interfere with my job."

5

"I told you I didn't care if you had tea and crumpets with Jesus as long as it didn't interfere with your job." Dan tossed the magazine with her first column from her 'Journey with Jesus' column — 'A Visit With Jesus'.

An artist's rendition of Jesus stared up at her from the page. Jesus had a slight smile on his face that she hadn't noticed before. Almost as if he was saying, I told you so.

She met Dan's glare. "It's not interfering. I wrote that on my own time from my own computer at home. There's nothing in the article that even links me with Global Entertainment."

"No, but I'm sure you used your contacts here to get the magazine space. How do you expect the people you work with here to react to something like this? It'll make them uncomfortable."

"I don't know. I'm hoping they'll want to

take their own journey with Him, I suppose. Or at least think about it."

His face flushed red.

Apparently that hadn't been the answer he was looking for.

"You're a vice-president. I can't have people thinking you're some sort of religious nu . . . religious fanatic. It's not the way we do business around here."

"Dan, I told you my visit with Jesus changed me. Changed my life. I'll not pretend it didn't happen."

"It's the brain tumors. They're doing weird thing in your head right now. Trust me, once they get fixed, you'll forget all about this Jesus thing."

"It's not the brain tumors, Dan. It was real. Jesus held my hand. We talked. He told me how much he loved me. Then Jesus gave me a gift of healing. A gift I plan to use."

He glared. "What are you even doing here? Your procedure is tomorrow."

"I needed to catch up on a few things so I'd be ready to hit the bricks hard when I get back on Monday for the Faith Now conference."

"Maybe you should take a little more time off than that. You've been through some really traumatic events recently. The accident. Then the tumors. I don't think you're ready to come back quite yet."

Was he firing her? Was that even legal? Of course, it wasn't. "What are you saying, Dan? Are you firing me because I wrote a religious article for a religious magazine?" She stood up and met his gaze.

"I'm saying I think your accident, and then the brain tumors, have taken more of a toll on you and your health than you realize. Take the rest of the month off and then we'll talk about when would be a good time for you to come back after that." He smiled. "Believe me, it has nothing to do with that." His finger jabbed at the magazine in her hand.

"I'll be ready on Monday."

"I don't think so."

"Dan, let's not play games. You can't fire me for writing a magazine article on my own time. Especially since it deals with religion and my religious freedom. Something guaranteed by the Constitution."

A flash of anger was quickly replaced with a fake smile. "Is that what you think? That I'm firing you? Not at all. I already told you I love your work. You're doing a great job. You've been invaluable since you got here. I'm just worried about your health. I want you to be in tip-top shape if you . . ." He paused. "I mean when you come back."

"Monday, Dan. I'll be back Monday."

"I'm still the boss, I'll call you in a month to discuss it. Marcus can handle the Faith Now conference for you. Please give him your materials." He headed away, but then turned back. "Of course, you'll have full pay and benefits while you're out sick."

She stared as he closed the door, not believing what had just happened. It was more than ridiculous, it was . . . unfair.

The moment Rachel got home she went in search of Cooper. She paced around his office as she explained what happened. "He can't fire me for this, can he?"

"Of course not. There's nothing in your contract that prohibits it. And he knows that. That's why the threat was veiled in so much concern about your health. There's no way he wanted to open his company up to a lawsuit. Some of his best clients are televangelists and religious concerts."

"It wasn't all that veiled. I knew exactly what he was saying. Stop talking about Jesus or you won't have a job. I don't understand why it bothers him so much. I'm good at my job. That's all that should count."

"Real life isn't all about the shoulds. I'm sure his plan is to give you a nice severance package and have you go away quietly."

"I don't see that happening." She paced

around Cooper's office once again, then stopped. "What do you think I should do? Should I stop writing for the magazine?"

"I'm certainly not telling you what to do. But I will tell you that it's not always easy or comfortable following Jesus. Vocal Christians have always been persecuted. It's really up to you."

"I sort of figured that's what you'd say."

"We can live on my paycheck without a problem so do what you want. Don't worry about the money."

"Aren't you sweet?"

"I try. I try."

Later that afternoon, she walked back into Cooper's office. "I just sent my second column to the magazine. I talked about the fact that Jesus gave me a gift. A gift he wants me to use. And I have no plans to disappoint him."

He grinned. "Good for you. I want you to use that gift, but you have a lot going on right now with your treatment. Maybe you should concentrate on that for the time being. Let the rest happen naturally."

"I can't exactly do that. I've been busy since I got home. I talked with one of my contacts at one of the networks who put me in contact with Mark Matthews."

Cooper arched his brows. "The expose

guy on TV?"

"He loved my idea for a show. In fact, we're working on them being present at my treatment. The idea is to pick three people for me to heal and follow them as well. This could turn into something amazing."

He sat back in his chair. "Wow. I didn't expect this. But then again I shouldn't be all that surprised. When you decide to do something, you don't spend a lot of time thinking about it. Or the ramifications." Cooper didn't sound excited. He sounded . . . worried.

"What do you mean? Ramifications?"

"I'm not sure, sweetie. But TV for your first attempt at healing? I don't know if that was the best idea you've ever had."

"Don't you believe in me? Don't you believe Jesus gave me the gift of healing?"

"Absolutely, I do. All I'm saying is TV might not have been the best idea. But you are who you are and I love you for that very reason. So if you think it's a good idea, I'm all for it. Take a little time to think about it before you decide if it's what you want to do."

"I don't need any time to think about it. I wouldn't have started the ball rolling if I hadn't thought it was a good idea. It's all about faith. So I'm stepping out in faith.

You can't walk on water if you don't get out of the boat."

"I doubt if Dan'll like a TV show that features you."

"Probably not, but a woman's got to do what a woman's got to do."

Nia had found a few more pieces that went together as Rachel talked, but the puzzle remained disjointed. "Wow. When you make a decision you really go for it."

"That's not always a good thing. But I'm definitely a doer, not a wait and see-er."

"I guess it all worked out because here you are, right? With your own little healing house."

"Not a healing house, the Puzzle House." Rachel touched a few puzzle pieces. "God is the healer. All I do is help you put the puzzle together."

"You keep talking about this puzzle like it's a miracle, or my life, or something. And God ain't got a miracle for me. I already told you that. When it comes to me He's all out of them." Nia touched her almost-bald head. "As you can see. But you know what? Go ahead and try to heal me. Do your thing. Let's see what happens."

"It doesn't work that way."

Nia's internal struggle played out on her

face. She wanted to ask something but didn't want to give Rachel the satisfaction. Finally she spoke. "Then how does it work? How do you heal people?" Her voice was sincere this time. Apparently hope had won.

"I don't heal people. God does. Jehovah Rapha. It's one of God's many names. It means the Lord your Healer." Rachel struggled up, then weaved her way to a tall floor lamp by the chairs. She turned toward Nia and lifted the cord. "Healing is a lot like this lamp. I'm just the cord. God is the power source. The light comes from the source, not the cord. If you don't turn the light on, there's still no light. You have to be the one to flick the switch if you want to see the light. Otherwise all that power sits there. Waiting for you to turn it on." She tapped the bulb.

Doubt flickered in Nia's eyes but hope shone, too. "How do I do that?"

Light flooded the room as Rachel turned the switch. "Faith."

"You're talking about faith in God, right?"

"Not just faith in God but faith in His love for you. Faith that He can and will heal you. Faith opens the way for miracles. Matthew 13: 58 even says, 'And he did not do many miracles there because of their lack of faith'. God is God, of course, and can do anything He wants in spite of us. But that verse shows us how important faith is. Especially when we want a miracle. Need a miracle."

Hope flickered in Nia's eyes. "God's never done anything for me and He ain't about to start now."

"God's done all kinds of things for you. Sometimes it's hard to recognize them. For instance, you have an amazing aunt who loves you very much. And you're here, aren't you? That's a start."

"A small one."

"Do not despise small beginnings." Rachel smiled. "That's in the Bible, too."

"You sure talk about the Bible a lot."

"That's because it's not just a book. It's the sword of God. And a sword is what we need when we're in a battle."

"I don't know about all that. I mean it was written so long ago. What's it got to do with my life now?"

"Remember when Jesus told me I had all I needed for my journey?"

Nia nodded.

"He meant the Bible but I'll tell you all about that later."

"Why not now?"

"Because it's out of order. I have to tell the story in the right order or I get confused." She tapped her head. "Brain tumors, you know. Gotta do it my way."

Nia giggled. "Go for it."

6

It was the day of her Gamma Knife treatment. Before they walked into the tiny building on the huge medical campus in Cleveland, she stopped in front of the small camera crew.

"Morning, Mark."

Mark Matthews was a well-known TV host for one of the leading networks. He did all sorts of stories, but his stories on the supernatural were his fans' favorite. When she'd contacted him, he'd jumped at the chance to tell her story on his show.

She'd had positive feedback from her magazine articles. People wanted to know more about God and about her experience. People needed healing. She'd wanted to help every one of them, but had to put it on hold for now.

Until she had her own treatment. And finished the show. Then she'd figure out how the best way to help other people.

She'd thought about it, but nothing was coming to her yet.

Of course, there was so much she didn't know. But she had no plans to stop writing for the magazine. Dan would have to deal with it. Or not.

Mark walked up to them. "Morning, Rachel."

They'd already done two pre-treatment interviews about her visit with Jesus. She'd tried to get the hospital to let her be filmed for the entire process. They'd refused, but had agreed to Cooper taking still photos inside the treatment area.

"How are you feeling today?" Mark asked.

"A bit nervous. It's not every day, someone puts screws in my head."

He laughed and pointed behind him at the tiny brick building. "I didn't expect the place to look like this, did you?"

"Not really. But they assure me it's a world-class treatment center. Another blessing that God placed me in a city where I could get the best treatment available." After several more questions, she took Cooper's hand and they entered the building. She had a few jitters, but nothing like she would normally have. God had answered her prayers.

She was surprised at how tiny the place

was on the inside as well. Her gaze swept the room. Two other patients and their companions sat in the chairs. There were only two chairs left for her and Cooper. Now she understood why they'd said no to a camera crew — the place was too small to allow for more than one visitor with each patient.

She smiled at the others. They all had to be worried.

As if reading her mind Cooper squeezed her hand and she gave an answering squeeze. She walked up to the receptionist. "Rachel Summers."

"Good morning, Mrs. Summers. I need your insurance card and a picture ID."

Rachel pulled them from her coat pocket.

A few minutes later, she sat beside Cooper. "I'm the last one in line. She wasn't sure how long of a wait it will be."

"Not a problem. We've got nothing else to do today, right?"

"Very funny."

He kissed her cheek. "That's my job. Keeping you calm and relaxed."

A nurse came out and called the first name of the day. The man stood up, gave his companion a thumbs up. "Let's get this show on the road."

The door shut behind him with a bang.

Please God, keep me in your peace. I can do this. The butterflies in her tummy settled and she was able to breathe again. Rachel smiled at the woman next to her.

"Is this your first treatment?" The woman asked.

Rachel nodded. "I'm a little worried about them putting the screws in my head."

"Yeah, but it sounds worse than it really is."

"How do you know that?"

"It's my second treatment. And hopefully my last."

"I have to have two treatments as well."

"So, you have NF2?"

"That's what they tell me." Rachel grimaced.

"Welcome to the club."

"From what I understand, it's a small club."

"That's what I hear, too."

"So . . . I don't mean to get personal or anything but how are you? Did the other treatment work?"

"Oh, it's OK to get personal. We should share information with each other when we can. I'm doing pretty good. I had some issues with my first treatment and had to be put on steroids for a short time. I lost a little more of my hearing and have some balance issues, but all in all, I'm not too bad."

Cooper asked a few of his own questions. They introduced themselves and by the time the nurse came out for the woman, they were chatting like old friends.

When it was her turn, Cooper was told he could accompany her to her MRI, then he'd be booted out.

"Another MRI?" Rachel asked.

"Procedure. Just to make sure there aren't any surprises when the doctor gets here."

They walked from one tunnel to another until they ended up at the MRI department on the other side of the clinic. After the MRI, they hurried through the tunnels once again. "I guess I did my workout for the day."

The nurse laughed. "Tell me about it. I do this six times a day. Twice for each of the three patients we have."

"Time to go." The nurse told Cooper as they entered the surgical area.

After taking a few pictures Cooper kissed Rachel on the cheek. "I'll be praying."

The nurse smiled. "So, I hear we're about to be famous. Some TV show or something?"

"Mark Matthews."

"Wow. That's pretty cool. Now you'll put on the halo. Then you'll have to wait for your turn to get the mapping done."

"Mapping?"

"That's what they call it. The computer will make an exact map of your brain and the tumor from every angle. After that, the doctor comes in and programs exactly what the Gamma Knife treatment is supposed to do. Depending on what they program in, your treatment should last anywhere from forty-five minutes to an hour and a half. sometimes, it takes up to two hours for the treatment. After that we take the halo off and you can go home after an observation period."

"Piece of cake." Rachel said with a nervous laugh.

The nurse patted her hand. "It's understandable to have the jitters — even to be afraid. But it will all be over in a few hours, and then the healing starts."

Healing. Rachel had chosen to be a healer instead of being healed. Did that mean the treatment wouldn't work? Was she going through all of this for no reason? Maybe, she shouldn't have agreed to the treatment so quickly. But the doctor hadn't acted as if she had a choice.

Dr. Tabb walked in with a group of people — his entourage. "Morning, Mrs. Summers. How are you feeling today?"

"Not too bad."

"Great. I've got a little group here with me. A few are medical students, and two are neurologists who are learning this procedure. Is that OK with you?"

"Sure."

"OK, I'm going to numb the spots where I'll put the screws in. As I put in the screws, you'll feel some pressure, but no pain. If you do feel pain, let me know. I'll get you more anesthesia."

"Sounds good."

After using a magic marker to mark the locations where the screws would go, Dr. Tabb inserted the first needle.

Rachel closed her eyes. She felt the pop as the instrument pierced through her skull. *Keep me in your peace, Lord.* She felt no pain, only an uncomfortable pressure as the screws were put in.

The doctor patted her shoulder. "See that wasn't too bad, was it?"

She took a deep breath, glad it was over. "You're right. I thought it'd be a lot worse."

"Everybody does. OK, so now we're putting the head gear on, then we'll lock you into the machine so your head can't move. Then I'll be back with the computer mapping exactly where we need the radiation to go. After that, you can go back out to the waiting room and eat something while we plan your treatment."

"Thanks, Dr. Tabb."

Two of his assistants came forward with a metal contraption. They slipped it over her head, then began to bolt it to her skull. Still not painful, but certainly not comfortable either. Once it was in place, they helped her lay back while they secured the halo to the machine.

"Would you like some music?"

"Sure."

"What kind?"

"Got any praise music?"

"Good choice."

Forty minutes later, they were back. After helping her to sit up, they helped her make her way to the waiting room.

Cooper jumped up. "Are you OK?"

"As much as I can be with this thing on my head." It was heavier than she'd expected and her neck already felt tired from the strain of keeping her head up.

"Are you hungry?"

"I'm starving." She hadn't been allowed anything before the procedure because of the anesthesia. "But let's get a few pictures first."

After Cooper helped her to a seat, he picked up the camera and snapped a few more. "For Mom and Dad."

"Lovely." She grinned.

"I'll go get the food in the car."

The other two patients were already back. One pinched off tiny bits of a sandwich and then slipped it in between the halo to her mouth. The other sipped something from a cup with a straw.

The treatment was painless. They put her in a machine much like an MRI and piped in music. Forty-five minutes later, the procedure was finished.

"Okie Dokie. All done." The nurse helped her to sit up. "I'll let you rest for a moment, then we'll get this thing off your head. Unless you'd like to keep it on as a fashion statement."

"Uh . . . probably not."

"Didn't think so." She smiled. "I know this is a tough day, but necessary."

"I know."

"Are you ready for me to take it off?"

Rachel nodded.

The nurse unscrewed the head gear. The fourth screw proved to be a tough one.

Rachel squeezed her eyes shut as pressure on her head was tugged back and forth until the screw finally loosened.

"OK, now I'm taking it off. It'll hurt, but only for a moment or two."

104

The head gear was lifted off her head. Her head exploded with pain. She moaned as she bent over. She couldn't breathe. Or think.

The nurse patted her. "I know it hurts but only for a minute or so. It won't last long. Keep breathing. Nice slow breaths."

It was the worst pain she could ever remember. Rachel couldn't even open her eyes. *Only a minute. Only a minute.* It seemed like an hour already.

The nurse reappeared. "Better?"

"A little."

"OK, you can go out to the waiting room and sit with your husband. I'll check on you in about fifteen minutes."

"Can you help me?" Rachel still hadn't opened her eyes — she couldn't.

The nurse led her out.

Cooper took her hand. "Are you OK?"

"In pain." She managed to answer. "Need to sit."

He guided her to a chair. "What's wrong?"

"Can't talk now."

He held her hand. "OK. I'm right here."

Another five minutes passed, the pain subsided somewhat. She was finally able to open her eyes.

Cooper stared at her, tears in his own eyes.

She gave a weak smile. "I'm better. The

pain's starting to go away."

"Are you sure?" Fifteen minutes later, he helped her to the car.

The pain was still there but bearable. Rachel held his hand. "I'm glad Mark Matthews didn't wait around for this part. I must look a mess."

"You're beautiful."

"You always say that."

"Because it's always the truth."

Thirty minutes later, he helped her into the house. "Want something to eat?"

"In a little bit, just let me lay down for a while."

"What would you like, sweetie? You name it, I'll fix it."

"I don't care."

"That doesn't sound much like you. You always care about what you eat."

"Not today I don't."

The next morning only the memory of the pain remained. And a mild headache. She moved to a sitting position in bed as the door opened.

"Breakfast in bed for my girl." Cooper grinned at her.

"You don't have to spoil me. I'm quite capable of eating downstairs."

"I know that, but I want to." He set the tray on her lap. "Fresh-squeezed orange juice, scrambled eggs, and croissants."

"Looks delicious. I'm starved."

He sat down on the edge of the bed.

She took a forkful of the Cooper's famous kitchen-sink scrambled eggs. They had a little bit of everything in them, thus the name. "Perfect."

"Are you feeling better now?"

"Much." She grabbed the croissant.

"The pain's gone?"

"I still have a slight headache. But very slight. Don't forget you need to clean the screw holes."

"I'll go get the alcohol now." When he came back, he asked, "So, what's on your agenda for today?"

"Mark is stopping by with bios on the three people he's chosen for me to heal. Then later this afternoon, I'll call and set up appointments to meet them in the next few days. And then I guess it will be time to show my stuff. To heal them."

"How will you do that?"

"I'm not really sure. Pray. I guess. Doesn't that make sense to you?"

"Sounds right to me." He grabbed her hand. "But if you're not up for it, then don't do it. You need to take it easy for a few days. The doctor said so. And it's not too late to back out of the TV thing."

"I'm fine. Almost as good as new. Still a bit of a headache but nothing like yesterday. You go about your day just as if I weren't here. Do what you need to do."

One of the reasons they'd been able to relocate to Ohio so easily was that Cooper could work from home. When necessary, he flew to headquarters.

He grabbed a croissant off her tray. "What will you do about your job? How do you see that playing out?"

"I don't know. I hate to quit. I love my job and financially speaking —"

"Finances aren't a problem, Rachel. I already told you that. We can live on my salary quite comfortably. If you want to quit work, you can."

"I just hate the thought of quitting. I worked so hard to be vice-president. And I really do love my job."

"True, but it seems as if God may have other plans for you."

"It seems that may be the case."

"What's Dan saying about the TV show?"

She set down her fork. "He doesn't know yet, but I'm guessing it'll put him over the edge. After his reaction to the magazine article, I hate to see what he'll think about the TV show. But they agreed to not mention where I work."

108

"I wonder what he'll say after you've healed these three people."

He had faith in her and her new gift even if no one else did.

Mark showed up at her house that evening. "All three have cancer — stage four." Mark handed her three manila folders, each with a different name.

Rachel opened the one on top. Only basic information, name; age; address. A quick glance showed the same for the other two. "Stage four?"

"Well, that shouldn't make any difference if you really have this gift of healing like you say. Does it?"

"No, but —"

"I want to be fair with you. But I sort of figured if I chose anyone less than terminal, the public could just put it down to luck or coincidence. You wouldn't want that, would you?"

"No, but —"

"Do you want to back out? If you do, I'd understand. I'll just take the footage I have and make it into a three-minute fluff piece. Is that what you want me to do?"

"No, but —"

"Good, then that's settled. I already have interviews set up with the three of them. For tomorrow. We'll film you meeting with them and doing whatever it is you'll do. After that, I'll keep tabs on how they're doing. In a month or so, we'll do follow-up interviews with them, and with you, of course."

"Tomorrow? That's not exactly what I had in mind. I wanted to meet with each of them first, and then you could come later and film us."

"I thought it would be better this way. No collaborating with any of them beforehand. That way my viewers can meet them at the same time you do."

After he left, she stared at the door with a frown. She'd wanted to meet with the patients before Mark filmed them. Panic coursed through her. Tomorrow. *Jesus, I don't know what to do.* She slid off the couch and onto her knees.

"I got a bad feeling about this guy." Nia looked up in triumph as she fitted two more pieces together.

"Yeah, well I could have used you back then. Too bad I didn't have that same bad feeling. But as I told you, back then when I got something in my mind, I just went ahead with it. Full throttle."

"So how bad was it?"

"Pretty bad. One of the worst experiences

110

of my life, actually. Almost as bad as having brain tumors."

"You know you'd think God would make it easier for you. Since He picked you to be a healer and everything."

Rachel picked up a plain brown puzzle piece. "You'd think. But it doesn't seem to work that way for most people. Or for puzzles. Take this puzzle piece." She held up the plain brown piece.

"What about it?"

"It's sort of ugly. Nothing pretty about it, but when you put it in the right place it becomes part of the beauty of the puzzle." She fitted the piece where it belonged as the bark of a tree. "Life is the same way. Unfortunately when we're going through the dark times, we don't always know how they fit into the puzzle so we can only see the ugly. It's only after the puzzle's finished that we see the ugly pieces were just as necessary as the pretty pieces."

"So what? I'm 'spose to be happy that I'm sick, or that my mama is a druggie, and left me with my Auntie?"

"Not at all. Only know that all your experiences, good and bad, are part of your unique puzzle. A puzzle that's very precious to God."

"Yeah, the last thing I am is precious to

God. Or anyone. I ain't precious. Believe me."

"Oh, yes you are. Whether you know it or not, you are very precious to me." Rachel met Nia's gaze.

Something softened in the girl. She gave a shrug. "Yeah, whatevs. So what happened?"

"Glad you asked."

7

Sandy Snoddy.

Sitting in her car, Rachel looked at the file one last time as she waited for Mark. Not that she didn't already know every word in it. She'd pored over all three files yesterday until she could almost recite verbatim every word in them.

Sandy had Stage IV breast cancer. She was thirty-seven, married, with two children. Nine-year-old twin boys. And she wasn't doing well.

All three of the people Mark had chosen weren't doing well, Hospice had been called for every case. But that was OK, nothing was too difficult for God.

Rachel smiled as she imagined each of them in a doctor's office with the doctor saying the word, 'remission'. How wonderful that would be for them. For their families. Then Mark and Dan and everyone else would become believers. They'd know Jesus really had given her the gift of healing.

She frowned as she thought back to the meeting with Mark. Yesterday's meeting had a different tone than the previous ones. Mark had been cooperative and friendly before. They'd seemed as if they were partners on the project. That appeared to have changed yesterday. It had seemed almost adversarial. Maybe he was just having a bad day.

It wouldn't matter after she proved she really had the gift to heal these people. Then people would listen to her. Give her respect. She closed her eyes, wondering how her life might change. Not that it mattered. It wasn't about her — it was about God.

Mark's van pulled in the drive behind her.

Closing her eyes, she prayed. "Please be with me, Jesus." Nothing happened. No miraculous nod from God that she was doing the right thing.

Mark opened her car door with a big smile. "Morning, Rachel. Are you ready to show your stuff? To show the world you are a healer?"

She forced a confident smile. "Absolutely."

"I'm not sure if I mentioned it yesterday, but I already did pre-interviews with them. So today we'll be filming you as you meet them, and then as you do your healing."

She'd thought this day was about the pre-interviews. He was testing her. But she was up to the challenge. "Well, it's fine with me. Remember you can film me meeting with them and leading up to the healing. But the actual healing part will be private."

He ran his fingers through his perfect hair. "No can do, sweetie. I need to film it all. Otherwise, how will we know what you did?"

"What I'll be doing is praying. And that part will stay private. That's between me, Sandy, and God."

"That's not what the contract says."

"I read the contract, Mark."

"Then you'll remember the part that says I have complete access to the patient and their medical care. As far as I'm concerned, you're part of their medical care so I want to see what you do. Film it."

"No." Rachel knew time and money had already been spent on this project. The network was supporting it. They wouldn't be happy with Mark if it fell apart at this stage. He wasn't the only one with the cards. She had a few to play herself. "Mark, I've been cooperative up to now. But I'm not backing down on this point. No cameras while I'm praying with them. If you aren't happy with that, then we can stop the whole thing right now."

They glared at each other.

Her pulse ramped up. She didn't want this to fall apart, but she'd promised herself she wouldn't cheapen her gift with TV theatrics. And she would stand by that.

"Fine, we'll do it your way. No cameras during the actual healing. If you heal them."

He didn't believe her? He hadn't ever expressed any doubt that he believed her story.

The door opened and an older woman with gray hair rushed out to meet them. Rachel put out a hand, but the woman hugged her instead. "Bless you, my dear. This is so wonderful. After we heard about your experience, we're sure you'll be able to heal my daughter. She's so very sick."

Rachel smiled. "Thanks."

"She's not having a good day today."

"Maybe we should come back another time."

"No. No. No. She needs to be healed now. She's so weak, I'm afraid if you wait another day or even a few more hours, she might . . ." She wiped away a tear. "Let's do it now. I'm sure that Sandy doesn't want to wait either."

Rachel walked into the room and was assaulted by the smell. She couldn't catch her next breath. She wanted to walk out of the room. No, not walk — run. Death was the only way to describe the smell.

A woman lay in a hospital bed. Her eyes were closed. She looked like a concentration camp victim. Her hair was gone and her skin had a peculiar color.

Rachel wasn't sure what she'd expected, but it wasn't this. This was too real.

This woman had two children, a husband, and a mother who loved her.

Rachel picked up Sandy's hand. Cold and lifeless.

Sandy's eyes fluttered.

Rachel felt a slight pressure in her palm. Her stomach twisted. And in that instant she knew what the outcome would be for Sandy. But this was TV, she couldn't just stand there and do nothing. She forced herself to sound cheerful. "Good morning, Sandy."

Another slight pressure on her hand.

Rachel took a deep breath, then introduced herself. She looked at the cameraman. "Time to go. This part's private." She glanced at Sandy's mother. "I'm sorry, that means you, too."

"Not a problem, dear." She hugged Rachel. "God bless you, my dear. God bless you."

And then the room was empty of everyone but Sandy.

Knowing it was hopeless, Rachel prayed with tears streaming down her cheeks, keeping Sandy's lifeless hands in her own. There was no response from Sandy. Nothing that showed she was even aware of Rachel.

Oh, God. I don't know what I'm doing. Why did I think I could do this? Why did I think I could heal anyone? There's nothing special about me. I believed Jesus. I still do believe Him, but this wasn't the right way. This was a mistake.

After fifteen minutes, she forced herself to stand up. With no sense of joy or accomplishment she stared at the sick woman. She'd done nothing here. Changed nothing. Hadn't helped the poor woman who seemed to be struggling for her next breath.

The cameras were up and ready to go as she walked out of the house.

Fresh air. Clean and living. Rachel didn't say a word as she made her way toward her car.

Sandy's mother ran up to her and grabbed her hand. "She'll be OK now, right? You healed her."

Rachel couldn't meet Sandy's mother's gaze. If the woman looked at her, she'd know the truth of what Rachel felt and knew. "I don't know. I can't say what God will do. I can only do my part. The rest is up to God. And Sandy."

Anger blazed in the woman's eyes. "Up to Sandy? What are you trying to say? You think she doesn't want to live? Doesn't want to beat this thing? She . . ." The woman shoved Rachel. "You're a fraud. I never should have agreed to this. You're just a fraud."

"I'm not . . . I'm not. I promise you I did my best. But it was too late." She was horrified. The cameras were rolling and saving every bit of this for posterity. She leaned closer. "You should go in. Before it's too late."

The woman opened her mouth to scream at her. But the full meaning of Rachel's words hit her. She turned and ran back into the house to her daughter.

Mark walked up with his ten-thousand watt smile. "Wow. That was intense."

Rachel stared at him.

It was obvious he was thrilled with all the footage he'd recorded.

"Well, let's get moving. On to the next one."

These weren't people to him just opportunities to make an entertaining show. What had she been thinking when she'd

119

contacted him? "I'm . . . I'm too exhausted."
And she was.

"So . . . what? You're going to give up on the other two?"

A scream came from inside the house.

Rachel closed her eyes.

Mark knew it as well. "You're just going to let that happen to the other two people. Without even trying to heal them. Not to worry, they aren't nearly as sick as she was. You might have a chance with them."

He'd set her up. He was manipulating her. He didn't believe in her gift.

Anger coursed through her. But who was she angry at? Mark? God? Or herself? "I . . . I can't. I'm just too exhausted."

"So you're admitting you were wrong?" His voice taunted her as the cameras kept rolling.. "That Jesus didn't give you the power to heal. That it was simply an hallucination you had while you were unconscious?"

Was it true? Had it just been an hallucination? She was so tired . . . she'd never experienced anything like that before. How was she supposed to react?

"So you'll just let them die?" Mark asked, his voice dripping with fake sincerity.

"Of course not." Hours later, Rachel pulled into her garage but didn't move. She had nothing left. Not even the energy to open the door and walk inside her house. The afternoon was a blur. She couldn't remember their names and their faces. What she said or didn't say was a mystery. Of course, she'd be able to relive every awful moment with the magic of film. As part of her contract, she'd been given all the raw footage. Her protection against selective editing.

The car door opened.

"Are you OK?" Cooper leaned down.

She shook her head.

He scooped her up, carried her into the house, laid her on the sofa and placed a hand on her forehead. "Are you sick? Need a doctor? I knew you shouldn't have gone out today. It was too soon after the surgery."

Again she shook her head. "Tired. So tired."

"Bad day, huh? You rest for a while. I'll get you something to eat. I'll bet you haven't eaten all day. Have you?"

As if food could cure what was wrong with her. She closed her eyes. Sometime later, the tantalizing scent of tomatoes forced them open. In the background, she could hear Christmas music playing even though Christmas was long past.

Cooper had placed a TV tray beside the

couch. Now he sat down a bowl. "Your favorite comfort food. Homemade tomato soup and my super-duper toasted cheese sandwich."

"Sounds good." She forced herself to sit up. She wasn't hungry, but she hated to disappoint Cooper.

"I know you're just humoring me, but that's fine with me. As long as you eat something, it doesn't matter to me why you're eating it."

She dipped her spoon in the creamy red concoction. After swallowing, she smiled. "You're right. I feel better already."

"I always am. Keep eating." He pointed at the sandwich. "And don't forget to eat some of that. You need the protein. I'll be back in a minute."

He came back with his own tray. After a few bites, he looked at her. "Would you like to hear about my day?"

She nodded.

He told her about his latest project and then stopped talking to eat his food.

Her brain couldn't focus, but she had to get it out. "I failed. The day was a complete failure. I don't know what I was even thinking. You warned me but I wouldn't listen."

"I'm sure it wasn't nearly as bad as you think."

"It was worse than I could think. I didn't help those poor people at all. I made everything so much worse."

"You'll feel much better tomorrow. And besides, you're supposed to be taking it easy. You only had your procedure a few days ago, you know."

"I know, but Mark had set everything up so I figured it would be all right. I felt fine yesterday."

"Just because they didn't cut you open doesn't mean you didn't have a major operation. The doctor told you that."

"I hear you."

"You want to talk about your day?"

She tore off a piece of the toasted cheese sandwich. "The one woman died while we were there. Right after I prayed with her. It was all so horrible. Her mother lost it. Call me a fraud."

"You're not any such thing. And I'm sure Matthews set you up. He must have searched a long time to find someone that sick."

"You think?"

"I do."

"Even if that were true, it's still my fault. I gave those families false hope. I made them believe I was something special."

"You are special."

"And now they hate God. It's all my fault. I wanted to come home after the first woman, but . . . he convinced me to see the other two."

"What happened with the other two?"

"To tell you the truth, I can't remember. I'm so . . . so exhausted. So confused. But at least they didn't die while I was there." Tears slid down her cheeks as she remembered Sandy's mother's scream. "But not to worry, I have the footage to remind me. I can't watch it now. Maybe tomorrow."

He put down his spoon and picked up her hand. "No matter what happened, you shouldn't feel as if you failed. God's still the one in control."

Shame overtook her as she heard Cooper's words. He was right. God was in control. Not her. She'd forgotten that — again.

8

"That TV man took you for a ride, didn't he? I knew that was going to happen." Nia shook her head. "Never trust those TV people. They don't care what they do if it means they get a good story."

"You're right, but I had to learn that the hard way."

"He was all nice until he got the contract signed, then he took over. Right? Did things his way. And that probably didn't work out so good for you. It sounds as if he made you look like a fool."

"That's an understatement."

Nia tossed a puzzle piece on the table. "This is a mess. I'll never get it together."

Rachel picked up several pieces. "It just seems that way because you're just going willy-nilly. Fitting a piece here and a piece there."

"Willy-nilly? What's that even mean?"

Rachel picked up the piece. "Willy-nilly

means just moving forward without thinking about it. Without a plan. Sort of like what I did with Mark Matthews. The TV guy. Take this puzzle for example. You've been trying but you haven't gotten very far. You have a goal just as I had a goal. I wanted to heal people, but being a willy-nilly person I jumped in with both feet before I even knew what I was doing. And disaster happened." Rachel moved the puzzle pieces around on the table.

Nia was watching her with interest.

Rachel held up a straight-edged piece. "Once you've worked a few puzzles, you come to know that you need a plan. Some people go by color." She touched a few of the blue puzzle pieces all bunched up together. "But I like to start with the foundation. The frame, if you will."

"How do you do that?"

"Everyone's different, but this is the way I work a puzzle." She ran her finger across the edge of a piece. She'd arranged several of the straight-edged pieces together. "I put all the straight edge pieces together first and then work from there."

"Hey look, these two go together." Then she found another piece that fit. And another. "You're right this is easier."

"That's where I went wrong that first

time. With Mark Matthews. I tried to use my gift but I didn't have the foundation I needed. But of course I didn't know that then. And the whole thing was disastrous from start to finish."

"Did you find it? The foundation, I mean."

"I most certainly did. But it wasn't easy. But then again nothing worthwhile ever is."

"Well, it should be." Nia muttered as she fit two parts together, almost completing one of the sides of the puzzle. "I mean what good is it to be a Christian if it don't make life easier?"

"Oh, it definitely makes like easier. But being a Christian doesn't mean we won't have problems."

"That really don't make sense. It can't be both."

"Sure it can. We still have problems, but God gives us the strength to get through them. Think about it. You know the story of the baby Jesus's birth, right?"

Nia nodded.

"So if anyone was ever blessed by God it was Mary. Right?"

"I 'spose so."

"But look at all she had to go through. Bringing shame on her family. Hurting Joseph. The long trip to Bethlehem while she was pregnant. Even having her child born in a barn and then she watched him die on a cross."

"Wow. I never looked at it like that before."

"Worthwhile isn't always easy. And building the foundation I needed for my own puzzle definitely wasn't easy."

"So how'd you do it?"

"Well . . ."

"All three patients are dead. Rachel Summers . . . charlatan or healer? I'll let you decide." Mark Matthews face disappeared as Cooper shut off the TV set and sat back. His expression changed to a grimace. "Well, that's over and done with."

"I have a feeling it's just getting started. I've been telling people what happened with those three patients. But seeing it on the show. Seeing their grieving families. Everyone'll hate me now."

"Not everyone. I don't hate you." He picked up her hand and held it. "You can't change what happened. All you can do is move forward."

"Move forward? With what? Sandy's mother was right. I am a fraud."

"I don't believe that for a moment."

"Well, I do. In fact, what I did caused more pain for the families. I made things

128

worse. And it sure didn't glorify God. I'm not a healer of anything."

"Well, then that's all that counts. If you believe it, then that makes it so." He stood up. He was always her champion. It sounded as if he was giving up on her.

"What do you mean?"

"Proverbs 23:7. For as a man thinketh in his heart, so is he. If you've decided you're a fraud, there's nothing I can do to change your mind." His voice challenged her. "So . . . it's up to you. Was your meeting with Jesus real or not? Did he give you the gift or not?"

"I didn't make it up. It really happened. I'm sure of that."

"Good. Now let's go to bed and forget all about this. Time to move forward."

She stood up but didn't move. "I can't face everyone at work tomorrow."

"Of course you can. And you'll do it with a smile on your face. You know why?"

She shook her head.

"Because I didn't marry a quitter."

The next morning Rachel pulled into her regular parking spot at work. Every person in there had probably seen the Mark Matthews show last night. It had been even more horrible than she'd expected. Mark hadn't given her any sort of break. He seemed to enjoy her misery. The scene with Sandy's mother calling her a fraud must have been shown at least ten times. Mark asked probing questions that she couldn't answer.

When the show was finished, she wanted to move to a cave.

Cooper had challenged her. "You have to face them. Show them that you believe Jesus gave you a gift." Brave words from the man who didn't have to go into that building today. But he was right.

She might quit this job in the end, but she wouldn't slink out with her tail between her legs. There was no shame in trying to obey God, even if it had been a disaster. When she felt strong enough, she opened the door and walked into the building. She made a point to smile at each person she walked past. "Good morning."

They all said hello but wouldn't meet her gaze.

Oh well, she'd get through this day somehow.

Dan walked in. "Good morning, Rachel."

"Morning, Dan."

He shut the door, and then sat down in a chair. "I'm sure you're feeling bad."

"About what?"

"I saw the show last night. I'm really sorry

130

that Mark Matthews put you in such a bad light."

"It was bad, but I'm over it."

"Good. Then you're done with this healing thing?"

"I didn't say that."

"You said you were over it."

"I meant the TV show, not the healing thing."

His face turned red and his eyes glittered with anger. But a moment later, he gave her a sweet smile. "Whatever you want to do is fine with me. As long as it's on your time, not mine. Do you have that Wheeler Conference report yet?" He'd only given it to her two days before.

"Of course, here it is." She handed him a file. "I'll send you a more in-depth report in a few days."

Even though Rachel had been back to work for several weeks, her duties had changed dramatically. Dan had insisted on her giving up her former duties until she was finished with her treatments. She still had the title of vice-president but she was no longer in charge of any of the upcoming conferences. Her new role was to review conferences after they were over. Examine all the details. Find out what worked and what didn't work. Then send the analysis to him.

Not once did he mention her faith. Not once did he act as if her new duties were a punishment. "That's great Rachel. Thanks. Have a great day today." He took the file and left her office.

The stress level in her job had dropped almost to zero. Which gave her lots of time to think about her failure. Guilt pressed on her. It wasn't about her. It was about God. But it was so easy to forget that. Especially since she'd done such a spectacular job of humiliating herself.

Tears filled her eyes. She'd been blessed with an encounter with Jesus but that seemed so long ago. Maybe she'd lost the gift He'd given because she'd messed everything up. Now she was too afraid to even say the words aloud. She wasn't sure she ever wanted to try again. "I'm sorry, Jesus."

No response. Jesus was probably done with her and she didn't blame him.

Fire alarms rang. There was a loud whoosh like a windstorm, and then sirens. Drums and music, as well. What was going on?

As she stood up, she swayed. She looked through the glass windows of her office. Everyone was hard at work. Holding on to the chair to keep falling, she waited. But the smoke alarm wasn't flashing.

Didn't anyone else hear it?

She was so dizzy she couldn't stand up. She plopped back down in her chair. Then realization dawned. The doctors had warned her that she might have some issues with her hearing, but they hadn't explained what might happen. Non-existent sirens blared. She needed to start on the emergency steroids they'd given her. Did she have them with her? She'd filled the prescription but it was still in her medicine chest at home.

Opening her drawer, she picked up her purse. She had to get home and get the steroids. She moved toward her office door but swayed. She grabbed for the desk but misjudged, landing on the floor on both elbows. Pain shot up her arms and into her shoulders. From her position on the floor, she looked at the outer office.

Nobody had noticed her fall. She needed help. She crawled to the door. Grabbing the knob, she managed to get upright. She stood still as the room around her moved. Closing her eyes, she waited for it to stop and opened the door. Her gaze landed at the nearest desk. "Alice."

Her dark-haired assistant twirled around. She jumped up. "Are you all right, Rachel?"

■ ■ ■ ■

Two hours later, Cooper scooped her up from the car and carried her into the house.

"I'm so sorry you had to come get me." Her voice was probably too loud but she could barely hear herself talk because of the noises in her head.

"Don't be silly. You certainly couldn't drive." He put her on the sofa. "Stay there. I'll go get the steroid pack and some water. Then I'll call the doctor."

The noise was unbearable. The room still spun so she laid down hoping that would help. The spinning sensation kept going and going.

Cooper leaned down and spoke with a loud voice. "Here's the water. I talked with the doctor's assistant. She said to take all six pills right now. She said you probably wouldn't sleep much tonight because of them but there's not much she can do about that. Tomorrow, you can space the pills out some. Try to take all of them by noon so you can get some sleep."

"Did she explain why I can't stand up by myself?"

He answered but she didn't understand.

"What? I can't hear you over the noises in

my head."

He wrote on a tablet sitting on the coffee table. He held it up. YOUR VESTIBULAR SYSTEM. He leaned down so his face was near hers. "The nurse said it was the vestibular system." He spoke each word slowly and clearly.

"Oh, that makes sense."

The afternoon and evening passed in a noisy blur.

Cooper sat holding her hand as he watched TV.

Every now and then she opened her eyes, but the noises in her head were so loud she couldn't hear the TV anyway. The spinning continued. Finally, she sat up. "Go to bed, Cooper. I'll be fine out here."

He looked doubtful. "I'm —"

"Please. I feel bad enough. Don't make me feel guilty by trying to stay up with me all night. Go to bed. At least one of us can get some rest."

He leaned down and kissed her. "You yell if you need me."

"I will, I promise."

When she was finally alone, the tears came. She'd chosen to be a healer rather than to be healed. But she hadn't understood what that meant at the time. And she wasn't a healer, either. All three of those people had died. The TV fiasco had not only humiliated her, but brought no glory to God. He must be so mad at her. Here she'd been given an awesome experience and a wonderful gift and she'd messed the whole thing up.

All her life, she'd been successful. Not that it had been easy, but she didn't mind hard work. And now the most important task in her life, and she'd failed.

Jesus had told her that it wouldn't be an easy journey, but he'd also told her that she had everything she needed. But she didn't have everything she needed. She didn't have anything. And she wasn't even on a journey any longer. She had no idea how to start again. And even if she did, no one would ever believe in her gift again.

The night dragged on, filled with self-pity and recriminations.

Finally, she dozed.

When she woke up, she held a Bible in her hand. Funny, she didn't remember getting it. She stared down at the Good Book.

Cooper walked in the room. "Hey, hon. How're you feeling?"

"Better, I think. The noise is still there but it's bearable now. And I can hear you a little better. The room's not spinning quite as much either. Guess the steroids are working. Of course, I haven't actually stood up yet."

Cooper looked at the Bible in her hand and smiled. "Decided to do a little reading, huh?"

He was much more the Bible student than she was. Early in their marriage, he'd try to get her in the habit of daily Bible reading, but she just didn't have the time. "Not really. I don't even remember getting it."

"Mmm. That's interesting."

She set the Bible down. "OK, here goes nothing." She stood up but toppled back onto the sofa. "Well, that didn't work well." She held out a hand.

Cooper helped her up.

She weaved her way up the steps, holding onto the banister. When she was on her way back down, Cooper stood at the bottom of the steps. She smiled at him. "Waiting to see if you need to catch me?"

"Sort of."

"Well, I don't know about you, but I find the timing of all this a little too interesting."

"What do you mean?"

"I didn't want to have to face everyone at work after that show, and now I can't go to work even if I wanted to. I wonder if I made myself sick."

"But you did go in and you did face them.

Yesterday."

"True. I did. I smiled and said hello to every person I saw. And you know what?"

"What?"

"Not one of them had the nerve to mention the TV show. Except Dan, of course. Even though I'm sure they all saw it." She grabbed on to his arm. "What do you think that means?"

"I'm not sure what you're getting at."

"I'm not sure either. All this happened after the TV show aired."

"The stress might have brought it on. Not that it wouldn't have happened sooner or later. But you know what the doctors say about stress."

"I guess."

"Are you hungry?"

"I'm so famished. I need food and right now."

"That's the steroids."

"Maybe so, but it doesn't make me any less hungry."

He laughed as he helped her into a seat at the kitchen island. A moment later, he handed her a strawberry-banana yogurt. "Start with this while I cook you an omelet."

"Sounds like a plan."

"So what did Dan say about the TV show?"

"Typical Dan."

After eating, she wandered back to the sofa for a nap. She picked the Bible up as she settled in. As her fingers traced the letters, she felt a sudden urge to read it. Opening it up, she browsed through the pages. If something caught her eye.

Hosea. She'd never even heard of that book. She looked down at the words. *Your fruitfulness comes from me.* As if God had put those words there just for her.

Finally she moved on. 2 Timothy 3:16. *Every Holy Writing which comes from God is of profit for teaching, for training, for guiding, for education in righteousness.* Rachel stared at the words. For teaching. For training. For guiding.

Those were the things a person needed to become a doctor. And those were exactly what she needed to become a healer. What she'd needed, she'd had all along. Jesus had told her that. He'd said she had everything she needed for the journey, but she hadn't known what he meant. Now she did. The Word of God. It was all there to teach her, to train her, to guide her. A spark of hope ignited. The journey with Jesus wasn't over. Rachel touched her Bible. In fact, it was just beginning.

She shuffled through the pages. Her pulse

spiked as she read 2 Peter 1: 3. *His power gives us everything we need for life and godliness through our knowledge of him who called us by his own glory and goodness.*

No wonder she'd failed. She hadn't taken the time to train. Or to gain knowledge of God. "Cooper. Cooper."

He came running down the stairs. "What's wrong? Are you OK?"

She wiped away happy tears. "Why didn't you tell me?"

Concern was replaced with confusion. "Tell you what?"

She held up the Bible. "About this. It's amazing. It's . . . It's just what I need."

He grinned. "It's what everyone needs. It just takes some people a little more time than others to realize it."

"Can you get me some index cards?"

Nia looked up from her puzzle. She had a good portion of the outside done.

Rachel smiled and touched the puzzle. "So you found your frame, huh?"

"Lot easier this way."

"The Bible became the foundation for my life. I had so much to learn and didn't even know it. I couldn't do anything without God. But with God, all things are possible."

"Is that why I'm really here? My auntie

knows I'm mad at God. It really upsets her when I tell her that. So she brought me to . . ." Her hand flung around the room. "To this place. So you could try to make me not be so mad at God."

"I'm just here to help you with your puzzle. That's all. What your puzzle becomes is up to you."

"So, like what? If I don't love God you don't want to cure me. Is that the deal?"

Rachel smiled. "That's not the deal at all. There's a verse in the Bible that talks about rain falling on the just and the unjust. The rain is God's blessing. He gives them to everyone, not just those who believe in him."

Nia stared for a moment, and then tapped her puzzle. The border was almost complete. "You're right. It's a lot easier by building a frame around it. But it's still hard."

"Life is hard."

"But it shouldn't be that way. God shouldn't make it so hard."

"I agree with you. It would be really nice if life could work that way." Rachel picked up a piece of puzzle and rolled it in her hand. "But it isn't like that. So God's job is to prepare us for our battles. If we get our own way over and over, we won't really be ready for the big battles."

"Well, the big battles shouldn't come."

"But they do. That's the way life is. Remember what I told you about Mary and Joseph? This world isn't a perfect place, Nia. And until we get to heaven, we all have battles. Little ones, big ones, and everything in between."

"So, what? After you started reading the Bible, everything fell into place? Then you could heal people."

"I don't heal people. God does." She pointed at the light. "Remember, I'm just the cord. God is the Power, the Light."

"OK, so then God started using you to heal people." She grinned. "Is that a better way to say it?"

"Much better, but that's not exactly what happened."

"Well, what did happen?"

Rachel smiled as she shook her head. "Sorry. That's it for now. I'll tell you more later."

"You can't just leave me hanging like that."

"Sorry."

Brandon walked in with a huge smile. "Hey, did y'all miss me?"

"Not at all, country boy. I didn't even realize you were gone."

"So the city girl says. I got a surprise for you."

"Well, I hope it doesn't have anything to do with fish. Because I saw you out by the pond a while ago fishing. I ain't cooking up no fish for you."

"I knew you missed me." Brandon winked. "You should have come out. I could have taught you how to do it. You'd have loved it."

"I don't think so. That's the last thing I'd want to do. Even if I could get to the pond."

"No pity parties allowed."

"Whatevs."

"Anyway. . . ." He picked something up from the hall. When he turned back he was holding a guitar. "Look what I found! Now you can play me a song."

She wagged her finger at him. "No way, country boy. I told you I don't play anymore."

"But you don't play any less, right?" He gave her a look "Or are you still having a pity party?"

"I am not, but . . ."

"Come on, play a little something for me. Go ahead."

"Don't call me a goat head."

He doubled over in laughter.

They were good for each other. It was nice to see both of them smiling. Rachel struggled to her feet. "I'll let you two work this out."

Nia strummed the guitar and began to tune it. "Where'd you get this thing?"

"Found it at the thrift store. I didn't know if it was any good. But you seem to be making pretty music with it."

"Hardly." She strummed a few notes. "But the sound ain't too bad."

"Come on. Let's see what you got."

She started playing a song. "If I have to play then you have to sing with me."

"That's a deal I can live with." He joined in with the chorus of 'Jesus Loves Me'. When they were finished, he smiled. "More please."

"Bet you can't guess this one." Her fingers strummed out a familiar tune.

"Easy peasy, city girl. 'Smoke on the Water'. Every guitar player knows that one."

"So you play too?"

"Not really."

"Not really means yes." She stopped playing and handed him the guitar.

He played a few notes and then sang. "Amazing Grace. How sweet the sound."

She wiped away tears. "That was beautiful, country boy. I think you bought that guitar for you. Not for me."

He handed it back. "Wrong. This is my

gift to you. Like Rachel says, when God gives you a gift you should use it. Music is your gift. So use it."

"What's the point? I ain't gonna live long enough to . . . to do anything with it. And it sure won't make me better."

"Maybe not, but it will make you feel better. I know it makes me feel better. Music lifts our soul to God." He grinned. "And there ain't nothing better than that, city girl."

"Then you play something. I'm tired and I'm going to rest while you sing to me." She lay on the sofa, her feet touching him.

"Well, OK. Your wish is my command. Here's a song I wrote. Want to hear it?"

"Absolutely."

Darkness and trouble
No joy
No peace to be found.
Only sickness and sorrow abound.
No one around but . . .

The God of Creation never forsakes.
He is the God of Abraham, Isaac, and
    Jacob.
He is my God
And He is so good.
His love endures forever and a day.

He is . . . Jehova Rapha
The Lord who heals.
The Lord who heals.

And nothing is impossible.
No nothing is impossible for my God.
His love endures forever and a day.

He is . . . Jehova Rapha
The Lord who heals.
The Lord who heals.

He changes the darkness to light.
His peace brings joy and delight.
He is with us day and night.
His love endures forever and a day.

His promises are real.
His promises are true.
And He will never leave.
His love endures forever and a day.

My God is . . . Jehova Rapha
The Lord who heals.
The Lord who heals.
His love endures forever and a day.

He is . . . Jehova Rapha
The Lord who heals.

The Lord who heals.
His love endures forever and a day.

She clapped. "That's wonderful, Brandon. Sing it again."

"You're just saying that to be nice."

She propped up on her elbows. "Country boy, I think you know me better than that. I am not nice. So . . . sing it again. Please."

9

When Nia opened her eyes from her nap, she was alone. The guitar sat on the coffee table. Sitting up she ran her fingers on the smooth wood. Brandon was so nice to have bought it for her. He didn't seem sick — had to be family issues.

Maybe he was only trying to make her feel better, but she had to admit he was cute. She stared at the pond through the windows. She really was a city girl, but it was pretty here at Puzzle House. Even if it was in the middle of nowhere.

She wouldn't admit it to Auntie but it wasn't all that bad being here, either. Maybe she could learn a few things from Rachel. And Brandon was fun.

"Did you have a nice nap?" Rachel asked as she came into the room.

"Sorry."

"For what?"

"I probably should have gone upstairs."

"No way. I loved hearing the two of you making such beautiful music. In fact, it got me to thinking. And I sure don't know why I didn't think of it before. We need more music around this place." She handed Nia a glass of juice.

"Brandon says music lifts our spirit to God."

"And I agree. I'll get some instruments. Maybe the Meeting Room will become the Music Room. What do you think?"

"Might be a good idea."

"After all, music does lift our souls to God. So are you ready to hear a little more of my story?"

It had been the worst four months of Rachel's life — and the best. Four months of being tired, but not being able to sleep for more than a few hours at a time. Four months of not being able to focus. Four months of constant sound, though the tinnitus had improved. The doctors wanted her to go in for a hearing test, but she didn't feel well enough. Her mind never stopped, thoughts spinning day and night.

She was also eating everything in sight and looking for more. The last time she'd stepped on the scales, she'd gained twenty pounds. Most of her power suits wouldn't fit her any more, but she couldn't go to work anyway.

Or anywhere else.

Rachel wasn't sure if her balance had improved or she'd just gotten used to it and made the necessary adjustments. What she couldn't get used to was the way her head felt when she stood up or walked or moved. It was as if she could feel her brain moving inside her head, a very odd sensation. Physically she was a mess.

But it had also been the best four months of her life. There was no worry about the future or what would happen to her. Joy filled her days at all that she was learning as she studied the Bible. Each time she picked up the precious book, her brain fog lifted. Her stack of index cards grew as she read and experienced God's presence. His peace. His joy. His love.

Cooper walked down the steps with suitcase in hand. "I really don't think I should go. I don't like leaving you alone like this."

"I'll be fine. You cooked me up that batch of vegetable soup and lasagna so I won't starve. And some cookies. I'll be sitting here doing what I do every day. Eating and sitting."

"But what if . . ."

"No what ifs. I'm fine, Cooper. Really. I

promise I'll keep the phone near me at all times, but I can't imagine why I'd need to call anyone. There's nothing for you to worry about. I'll spend most of my time studying the Bible and eating."

"How's that going? About ready to step out of the boat again?"

"I feel as if I could study for the next twenty years and still not be ready."

"That might be how you feel, but I'm not sure if that's God's plan. I have a feeling He has other ideas." He paced around the room then turned back to her. "I'll tell them I won't be attending next —"

"You'll tell them no such thing. I mean it, Cooper. I won't have you giving up your life because of my health."

"Well, we'll see about that."

He bent down to her.

Her arms went around him. She hugged him tight.

A small gasp came from Cooper.

"What's wrong?"

"Nothing." He took a step away.

"That didn't sound like nothing. Did you hurt yourself?"

"I cut myself out in my workshop the other day. A very small cut. Nothing for you to worry about."

"I'll be the judge. Let me see it."

He kissed her forehead. "Sorry. I wish I could, but no time. Airplanes wait for no man."

"Cooper."

"Later, my love."

The moment the door shut, loneliness crept in. "Stop being a baby, Rachel." Life couldn't stop for everyone just because her own had. She slumped back in her chair. Her eyes closed as she dozed.

Sometime later the phone rang.

The phone was on the far end of the glass coffee table. If it was Cooper and she didn't answer it, he would panic. She jumped up from the sofa. As she reached down she slammed into the coffee table, which collapsed under her weight. With a moan, she pressed answer. "Hello."

"Where were you? What happened? You don't sound good."

Sprawled on the floor and surrounded by pieces of shattered glass, she forced a normal tone. "I wasn't as close to the phone as I should have been." There was no way she would tell him she'd just crashed through the coffee table. He'd be on the next flight home. "How was your flight?"

"Not bad. Just checking in with you."

After they hung up she crawled to the couch and managed to climb onto it. Completely exhausted she stared at the mess. Her index cards were scattered amidst the glass. Picking up one, she read the words. *Let the weak say they are strong.*

"I am strong." She glared at the mess. She'd clean it up . . . later. As the evening progressed, she'd pick up a few pieces of the shattered glass on her way to somewhere else. By bedtime, most of the larger pieces were in the trash. Now to find the energy to get the sweeper. That would have to wait until tomorrow. Maybe she'd feel better. "Yeah right." A positive attitude only went so far. The next morning Rachel sat on the couch, thinking about vacuuming when the phone rang.

"Mrs. Summers."

"This is she."

"This is Raul Mendez. I work with Cooper."

"What's wrong?"

There was a pause. "I know you haven't been feeling well, but I thought you should know . . ."

Her stomach twisted.

"Cooper collapsed this morning at a meeting and was rushed to the hospital. I'm here with him now."

She couldn't breathe. Finally, she managed to ask, "What's wrong with him? What happened?"

Heart attack? Or stroke?

"The doctor said he has some sort of blood infection."

"Infection? From what?"

"The doctor said from some cut he had. The problem is the infection went into his blood. He used the word sepsis. He's very concerned."

"Let me talk to Cooper."

"I can't."

"But I need —"

"The last time I saw him, he . . . wasn't conscious."

Not conscious. Sepsis. This sounded really bad. Very serious. "OK, I . . . I . . . I need to think a moment. Can you call me back in a little bit?"

"Of course."

"In the meantime if the doctor tells you anything else, call me." She took a deep breath. "And thanks for being there with him."

She slumped onto the sofa, staring at the tiny shards of glass that still littered the floor. "What should I do?" Of course she had to go to him. She couldn't let Cooper be there sick and all alone. But she could barely walk. One of her favorite verses floated through her mind. "I can do all things through Christ who strengthens me." She stood up. "Even get to Atlanta. Somehow."

"That sounds pretty bad." Nia said, her puzzle forgotten.

"Bad doesn't even come close to what I experienced. It's been years ago, but I can close my eyes and be right back there. How I felt — physically and emotionally. It truly was one of the most horrible days of my life. But I had to get to Atlanta. To be with Cooper."

"So you could heal him, right?"

"Truthfully, I wasn't thinking about that. I had to be there with Cooper. He was my husband and I loved him. I didn't want him to be alone."

"So what happened?"

"It was bad enough to have my mental confusion, my low energy, and the fact I couldn't walk in a straight line at home. I hadn't been out of the house in months by myself. And now I had to get to the airport, fly to Atlanta, and then get to the hospital. It was overwhelming."

"But you healed him? Right?" Nia said once again. "So did he live? Did you heal him?"

Rachel pointed at the lamp. "Remember

only God heals."

"Yeah, Yeah, I remember. So did God heal him?" Even as she asked the question, Nia knew what the answer must be. She'd been here three days and not seen a husband. Hadn't even heard anyone talk about Cooper. "Never mind. You probably don't want to talk about it."

"Oh, but I do want to talk about it."

10

Rachel stood in the middle of her living room. She had to get to Cooper before . . . well, she wouldn't think about that. She started up the steps to pack a suitcase. Halfway up, she stopped. It would be difficult enough to maneuver through airports and hospitals in her physical condition. There was no way she could do it while lugging a suitcase. She'd have to worry about clothes later.

She called for a cab. While she waited, she called an airline for reservations. By the time she arrived at the airport, she didn't think she could take another step. "I can do this. I can do all things through Christ who strengthens me," she whispered.

And God would help her.

An airline employee was helping people check in their baggage at the curb. The woman gave Rachel a perfunctory smile.

"Would you like to check your baggage here?"

Rachel shook her head. "I don't have any . . . I . . . I need some help. I'm not feeling well. I have brain tumors and I have to get to Atlanta. My husband is . . ." To her horror, tears leaked out her eyes. She took a deep breath. "Out of town. Business. Got sick. My husband's in the hospital. I have to get there."

The woman's eyes widened. "Did you say you have brain tumors? Do you need me to get a doctor? Or an ambulance for you?"

"Not me. My husband. Very sick in Atlanta. I have to get there."

The woman's smile was replaced with real concern. "How can I help you?"

"I . . . I guess I need . . . I need. I don't know what I need. I just know I have to get to my husband. He's very sick." Rachel handed the woman her flight information. "This is my flight."

"Take a deep breath." The woman patted Rachel's arm. "Don't you worry. I got your back on this. Hold on." She picked up the phone. "I need someone to escort one of our passengers. It's an emergency."

Four hours later, a cab pulled up to the hospital in Atlanta. The cab driver looked back at Rachel. "Are you sure you don't need help getting in?"

"Thanks, I can do it." She handed him two twenties. "Keep the change. Thanks so much for all your help."

Using her newly-purchased cane, she hobbled into the hospital. The airport employee had been more than true to her word. Not only had a wheelchair appeared out of nowhere, Rachel had an assistant with her to make sure she got to where she needed to be. When the flight was over, there was another attendant who made sure she got a cab.

There'd be several thank-you notes sent later. But she needed to get to Cooper. There'd been no change in her husband's condition the last time she'd talked to Raul. He wasn't responding to the antibiotics and still wasn't conscious.

According to Raul, the doctor was very concerned. That spoke volumes. Doctors didn't usually voice their worries.

She'd spent her time on the airplane in deep prayer. She'd never prayed so long and so hard for anything in her life. Cooper was her life. If he died . . . well, she couldn't even think about that right now.

Rachel tottered up to the reception desk. After she explained who she was looking for, the woman told her he was in ICU and the directions to get there.

Rachel held up the cane. "I need a little help. I'm not feeling so well myself."

A few moments later a young man wheeled a wheelchair toward her.

Rachel collapsed in it. "Thank you so much. I don't think I could take another step right now."

He patted her arm. "No problem, ma'am." After several turns, he brought her to an elevator. "Almost there. ICU is on the third floor."

She stood up. "I'm feeling stronger now. I think I can get there on my own."

"I don't mind taking you up. It's not a problem."

"Thanks, I can take it from here. And thank you so much."

As she stepped off the elevator, she was in a waiting room and near a reception desk. "I'm Mrs. Summers. My husband's been admitted here. Cooper Summers."

The woman nodded as her fingers flew across the keyboard. She looked up. "I'll notify the doctor that you're here. I'm not sure how long it will take before she can talk with you. Go ahead and have a seat."

Before she could move to a chair, a man in a charcoal gray suit approached her. "Mrs. Summers?"

She nodded.

"I'm Raul."

"Have you been in to see him?"

"Not since the emergency room. Only family's allowed to visit in there, but I didn't want to leave before you got here. The doctor was out about fifteen minutes ago. Said his condition was stable but not improving. I told her you were on your way."

"Thanks so much for being here with him. If you have other things to do, don't feel bad about leaving. I understand."

"Cooper's a great guy. He'd do the same for me. And I have no other place to be right now. I'll wait here with you. Are you hungry, do you need something to eat?"

She held up a bag. "I bought a few things. I'm on steroids and when I need food, I need food." Her gaze fell on a young girl sitting alone across the room. Rachel couldn't see her face because her blonde hair covered it as she rocked back and forth, her shoulders heaving with sobs. Rachel leaned over to Raul. "I'll be back in a minute." She walked over to the young girl. "Hi."

The girl looked up. Her puffy red eyes grew wide. "Hi."

"Are you OK? You seem to be alone."

"Oh . . . my mom got hit by a car. She's

really hurt." Big tears rolled down her cheeks. "I think . . . I think she's going to die. There was so much blood. My dad's on his way."

"Oh, I am so sorry, sweetheart." Rachel sat down. "What happened?"

"It was awful. We were walking across the street when this car came straight at us. I saw the car coming but I froze. I just stood there. A woman ran up and pushed me out of the way. I fell down. I saw the car hit them. They both got hurt. Really hurt. The woman's pregnant. I don't know what's going to happen to her or her baby." Tears dripped down her chin.

"Can I pray for you and your mom?"

"And the pregnant woman, too? They saved me. They both saved me. Now her baby might die."

As Rachel prayed, the girl clung to her hand.

The girl was sobbing. "I can't thank you enough."

"Lori." A man ran from the elevator to the young girl. "Are you OK?"

"I'm fine. But Mom. She's really hurt, Daddy. The doctor said . . ." She collapsed in her father's arms.

As his arms went around his daughter, Rachel backed away. Before she could leave, the girl grabbed her hand. "This nice woman was praying for Mom and the other woman who saved me. The pregnant woman. She saved me, Daddy."

The man looked at Rachel and gave a half-hearted smile. "Thank you so much."

Rachel nodded and walked back to her seat.

"Cooper told me what an amazing woman you are. I guess he wasn't exaggerating. You gave that girl hope. I could see the change as you prayed with her." Raul smiled.

A doctor walked out from the double doors. She passed Rachel and walked to an older couple holding hands. "I'm sorry. It looks as if the colon cancer's back. And it's spread."

"But he's so young. Only twenty-nine."

"I'm sorry."

The man looked at the doctor. "Treatment?"

The doctor shook her head. "It's too late. Now, it's about making him comfortable."

The woman sobbed as she clasped her husband's arm.

Rachel looked away, not able to take any more pain in. With closed eyes, she prayed for the young man and his family.

A woman walked out towards her. "Mrs. Summers?"

She used the cane to help her to a standing position. "That's me."

"I'm Dr. Zuchak."

"How's my husband?"

"Let's go into one of the conference rooms and talk."

Rachel's heart fluttered. That didn't sound good at all. She looked over at Raul. "If you want to come in that's fine with me."

"I don't want to intrude."

"You aren't."

The three of them walked into a small room.

"Your husband has an infection in his bloodstream. And it's serious. Very serious. He's not responded to the antibiotics at all."

"Should he have by now?"

"In fact, his vitals have worsened in the last half hour. Do you know when he got the cut?"

"I don't. I . . . I've been sick. Haven't been paying too much attention to anything. I should have known about —"

"No, it's not your fault. I wasn't accusing you. I just wanted to know when the infection was introduced into his system."

"Does it make a difference?"

"Not really. Not at this point."

"What do you mean? Not at this point?"

"I'm sorry. He's just not responding. I

164

think you have to prepare yourself for the worst-case scenario. If there's anyone else you need to contact . . . you should do it."

Raul's hand tightened around hers.

She wasn't sure she could breathe. "Are you saying he's going to die?"

The doctor nodded. "It's a possibility."

"It's not a possibility. He's not going to die. He's not."

"I'm sorry to say so, but it's a very real possibility. We'll keep him on the antibiotic drip and hope for the best."

"Hope for the best? It sounds as if you've given up."

"It's not that I've given up, there's nothing else to be done but wait, and see if he starts responding to the medication."

"Except pray," Rachel said.

"Of course, if you believe in that sort of thing."

"I do. I want to be with my husband."

"Visits are for family only. Ten minutes every four hours. I'll take you to him."

Ten minutes was unacceptable but this wasn't the time for Rachel to argue. She had to be with Cooper. She'd find a way to stay in there. As she followed behind the doctor, she whispered to Raul. "If you need to go, that's fine. I'm not coming out anytime soon. I'm staying with him."

He chuckled. "I do believe that. But I'll be out here. Is there anyone else I can call for you?"

She shook her head.

The doctor hit a button that opened double doors. "He's in bed four. Don't expect him to respond to you. But feel free to say what you need to say to him."

Rachel gasped when she saw Cooper. He seemed to have aged overnight, so pale and frail. He reminded her of Sandy. She closed her eyes, swaying.

Arms touched her shoulders. "Are you all right?"

"I'm fine," She said, opening her eyes and going to her husband.

"Well, did he make it? Did Cooper die? What happened?"

"Patience, my sweet girl. You have to let the story unfold, the same way you have to do the puzzle. One piece at a time."

"Oh, you and this puzzle. I don't know how putting together one stupid puzzle could be all that important anyway."

"And yet it is." Rachel smiled. "And I think you know that. You just don't want to admit it. Yet."

"It's just a puzzle. It don't mean nothing special."

"Are you sure about that?"

"Pretty sure. Well . . . tell me what happened."

The sheet was tucked around Cooper and his hands lay at his sides. Helplessness threatened to overtake Rachel. *Let the weak say they are strong.* "I am not helpless. I am strong."

She picked up his hands, hot with fever. How could he be that hot and yet so pale? She leaned in to kiss his cheek. "Cooper. I'm here. I'm with you. I love you." Still holding his hand, she fell to her knees.

A nurse walked over to her. "Ma'am? Are you OK?"

"I'm fine. I'm praying."

A shocked look was on her face as she backed away. "Oh, sorry. I didn't mean to interrupt."

"You weren't interrupting. Thanks for checking on me."

With her free hand, Rachel opened her purse and pulled out her stack of index cards. She read the first one aloud. "Psalm 94:18. 'When I said my foot is slipping, your mercy and loving kindness, O Lord, held me up." Another card. Mark 11: 12. "Therefore, I say to you whatever things you ask when you pray, believe that you receive

167

them and you will have them." She closed her eyes. After a moment, she opened them. "I believe your words, God. I'm asking you for a miracle. I know you will heal my husband today, and I thank you for that."

Index card after index card. Bible verse after Bible verse.

Ten minutes came and went.

Nobody told her to leave.

So she didn't. Instead, she kept reading her cards and praying and thanking God for His goodness, His love, His power, and His mercy. When her knees hurt so bad that she couldn't stay in that position any longer, she moved to sit, still on the floor, but holding Cooper's hand.

Suddenly, the chill of the ICU room was replaced with a warmth. But it wasn't just warmth, it was peace. It spread throughout her body. From her heart to her arms and legs. Then to her toes and then her fingers. Then the heat intensified. Tears of joy streamed down her face.

God was here in this place.

More index cards and more praises. Gradually, she became more aware of what was going on around her.

People were moving around. Talking. Laughing.

"Hey, what's going on? It's getting hot in

here," a nurse spoke.

"Is the thermostat broken? Feels like it. Call maintenance. Tell them we need them we need them to get the temperature right. Stat."

More heat flowed through her to Cooper. With tears in her eyes, Rachel praised. "Thank You, God. Thank You, God." As she struggled to stand, a slight pressure squeezed her fingers. Using the bed as an anchor she pulled into a stand. The pressure on her fingers grew stronger as she straightened up. Her gaze flew to Cooper.

"Hi, beautiful." His eyes were open and his voice was weak, but it was the most beautiful sound she'd ever heard.

She leaned down and kissed him. "Hi, yourself."

"How did you get here?"

"God."

They whispered I love you's to each other.

A nurse walked in. Her eyes were bright with unshed tears. She touched Cooper's arm. "How did I know he would be awake when I walked over here? I don't know who you are, sweetheart, but you called God down from the most high and brought Him here."

"He's better."

"Not just him. Everyone in this room."

Rachel focused on her surroundings. Nurses and doctors were rushing around. Patients were sitting up, smiling and laughing.

Rachel's gaze met that of a young woman, obviously the mother of the young girl she'd spoken with earlier. They looked so much alike.

She mouthed the words, 'thank you' to Rachel.

Rachel pointed upwards and said aloud, "Not me. God did this."

"I had one of my migraines and it's gone now. And you know what; I don't think I'll ever have another one." The nurse's eyes were leaking tears. "I never thought I'd see a miracle, but I did today. You gave everyone here a miracle."

"Not me. God."

The nurse grabbed her free hand. "I can't wait to have the doctors check on him." She pointed at a young man. "When he comes back cancer-free, even they'll agree it is a miracle. I gotta go. I got people who need to get in here with their loved ones. Thank you so much."

Rachel opened her mouth but before she could say anything, the nurse spoke again. "I know. Not you. God. Still I don't think this would have happened if you hadn't been here today."

Rachel wouldn't argue with that.

The nurse rushed off

In the corner of the room, a commotion started. "We need a doctor. Now."

Cooper tugged her hand.

She turned back to him.

"I disagree."

"You disagree with what, sweetie?"

"It's like the time in the Bible when a Roman authority asked Jesus to heal his servant. As Jesus got ready to go to the man's house, the Roman stopped him. And said he knew that Jesus didn't have to be in the same place to heal his servant. Jesus commended him on his faith. And the servant was healed."

Rachel processed that, then leaned over and kissed Cooper once again. "Are you saying I didn't have to go through all I went through to get here? I could have done it from the comfort of my home?"

He nodded with a silly grin.

"Because you really have no idea what it took for me to get here."

"I have a little idea of what it must have been like."

"I'm sure you do. I'm just teasing. There was no way I wasn't coming to be with you. I just . . . I don't understand."

"What don't you understand?"

"What was the difference between this time and the last time? I just don't get it."

"Really? And you're so smart. I can't believe you don't see it."

"Well, I don't. Can you enlighten me?"

"I can." He crooked a finger and she moved closer. As their lips met, she savored the moment. When they parted, he smiled at her. "Love made the difference."

"Love." Nia looked at her.

Rachel nodded. "Love. When Cooper said that word it was like all the puzzle pieces finally fit."

"Unlike my puzzle." Nia's voice was rueful.

"It's getting there. You're doing a great job."

"I still have a long way to go."

"And all the time you need to finish your puzzle."

Hope flickered in Nia's eyes. "You think so?"

"I can't tell the future, but I do know you'll have all the time you need to finish your puzzle. We all do. It's just some puzzles are finished sooner than others."

Tears welled up in Nia's eyes.

"Jesus talks about love a lot but the other

parts of the Bible do as well. Our heart is very important to God. That's why I have the verse written all over The Puzzle House. The Bible says faith, hope, and love are all important, but love is the most important."

"That's what the sign in the entrance says. Why is love so important?"

"Good question. I'm no theologian but this is what I've come to understand in my own life. Faith is about believing in God. Hope is about believing that his promises are true for everyone, including yourself. But you can't have the faith and hope if you don't believe God loves you. And that's why love is most important."

Nia wasn't looking at her. Her voice was soft when she spoke. "I don't think God loves me."

"Because you're sick?"

Nia nodded but said nothing.

"Do you see now that God does love you?"

"Maybe a little."

Rachel smiled. "That's a good start. Part of loving God is about sharing God's goodness with other people through your own actions so they can have that same faith, hope, and love, too. It continues the cycle. I receive God's love. Then I share it. And then that person shares it. And so on and so on."

Nia tapped the puzzle pieces. "Kind of

173

like this puzzle. All the parts are needed, but some pieces are a little more important than the others."

Rachel grinned. "I think you're turning into a great little puzzle worker."

"I don't know all about that. So what happened?"

"Oh, you mean after Cooper was healed."

"Are you talking about me?" Cooper walked into the room.

"You're back." Rachel jumped up and hugged him. "I didn't expect you until later today."

"Got finished early so I thought I'd surprise you."

"I hope that means you're planning on cooking for us. Poor Nia and Brandon have had to put up with toasted cheese sandwiches for the past three days."

"So this is Nia?" Cooper turned to her. She nodded.

"I'm so glad to meet you. Rachel couldn't stop talking about you before I left. She was so excited about you coming."

"Really?"

"That shouldn't surprise you. I'm sure she told you that you're special."

"I just figured it was something she says to everyone."

"That's because . . ." Cooper jumped in

and they both said, "Everyone is special."

Nia giggled. "Do you guys do that a lot? You know, finish each other's sentences."

"Sort of." Cooper told her. He walked over and looked down at her puzzle. "Looking good, Nia. I can tell you've been working hard."

"There ain't much else to do but work on it. After all, I'm in the middle of nowhere."

"Not much to do? Are you kidding me?" He grinned. "Haven't you been out to see the animals? Or go fishing in the pond? Or take a nature walk?"

"Go fishing?"

"Rachel, I cannot believe you've kept this poor girl cooped up in here for days."

"But —"

"But nothing. I had a feeling that might be the case so I invited someone to stop by."

"Hi, Grandma." Her grandson walked in. He leaned down to hug her.

"This is my beautiful grandson, Jarrod."

"Grandma, I keep telling you boys aren't beautiful."

"But you're beautiful to me. And you can't stop me from saying it. And you know why?"

"Because you're my grandma." Jarrod grinned, and then looked at Nia.

"So, Jarrod, I take it that you and your granddad conspired together."

"Well, Grandpa called and asked if I'd pick him up and not tell you about it."

Rachel grinned. "Keeping secrets from your grandma."

Jarrod pointed at Cooper. "His fault, not mine. So, Nia, are you up for a horse ride?"

"On a horse?"

"That's usually how you do it."

"I don't know. I never been on no horse before. And . . . and I'm . . ." She touched her wheelchair. "It's sort of hard for me walk much right now."

"Not a problem. I can push that thing to the barn and then help you on the horse."

"On a horse?"

"Yeah, that's the way you ride one. What do you do with horses?"

"Nothing."

"I love horses. Mindy will be perfect for you. She's so sweet and gentle."

Nia's chin jutted.

Here comes some of her attitude. Rachel sent a quick, silent prayer.

"I don't need sweet and gentle. I'm not afraid of no horse."

"That means you are afraid of them. You used a double negative. And everyone knows that makes the sentence just the opposite of what you meant."

"Fine. Then I ain't afraid of any horse."

"Good. Then let's go."

Nia looked at Rachel. "But I want to hear what happened. At the hospital. Especially with that guy with cancer. And the pregnant lady."

"I'll tell you all about them later. You go have some fun with Jarrod. Brandon's probably out there somewhere. I'm sure he'll enjoy seeing you on a horse."

After the two had left, Cooper hugged her again. "How's my favorite girl?"

"She's just fine."

"You look tired?"

"I'm fine. Just been busy with Nia and Brandon. Haven't had time for my naps."

"I'm sure. So what's she like?"

"She was really angry when she got here. But I've seen a change over the past few days. God is working in her. She really is a special young lady."

He gave her a sharp look. "How special?"

"Time will tell, but I'm thinking very special."

"Where's Annie?"

"She went home a few days ago."

"What did she decide?"

"She's moving to a facility. Her daughter was a bit upset but Annie convinced her that was what she wanted, so she agreed."

"Excellent." He nodded. "Now, I want you to go rest while I fix dinner. I wonder what Nia might like."

"But you just got home. You're the one who needs to rest."

"I'm fit as a fiddle. And I've missed my kitchen."

"And your kitchen's missed you." Rachel said fervently.

11

Rachel held on to the banister as she made her way down the stairs. The nap had only managed to make her more tired.

Laughter and giggles were coming from the kitchen.

She'd hoped the two would get along with each other. That would make things easier. For both of them. She forced a smile as she walked in.

Nia was sitting at the kitchen island as Cooper attempted to twirl pizza dough with his hands. He winked at Rachel. "Hey beautiful, did you have a good nap?"

"Lovely. How was your horse ride, Nia?"

"Uh, well, actually it didn't happen."

"Really? Why not?"

"I sort of chickened out. But Jarrod said he'd be back tomorrow to try again. I did pet Mindy. And he's right, she is sweet. She has the most beautiful brown eyes. Country boy thought it was the funniest thing ever when I wouldn't get on the horse. But what do I care what he thinks?"

"Just ask him to see how he'd do taking the bus from your house to the mall."

Nia giggled. "Yeah, I have to do three transfers."

"He probably doesn't even know what a transfer is." Rachel added. "I haven't been out to see the horses in a while. Maybe I'll go with you tomorrow." She pointed at the flour-covered kitchen island. "Quite the mess."

"We're making pizza." Cooper said.

"Six of them." Nia chimed in.

"Six? There's only four people here."

"Because Jarrod's coming and bringing his parents, too." Nia looked at her. "I didn't know you had any kids. You didn't tell me that before."

"That's because I haven't got to that point in the story yet."

"So as I finish this, why don't you finish telling Nia about what happened in Atlanta?" Cooper twirled the pizza dough.

"Still want to hear?"

Nia nodded.

The doctor walked up to them. "Well, I can't believe it. But his infection is completely gone according to the blood tests.

I'll release him tomorrow as long as his blood work comes back clean again. I just . . . I can't believe it."

"That is great news. God is so good." Cooper told her. "Thank you so much, Doctor."

"I don't know why you're thanking me. The antibiotics weren't working, and then you were just better." She turned to leave, but then came back. "The staff in the ICU are all abuzz, as you can imagine. They're saying you healed every person here today."

Rachel smiled. "God heals not me. But is everyone really better?"

"Everyone."

"Including the young man with the colon cancer?"

"I can't give you specifics because of privacy laws. But I'll say it again. Everyone in this room was healed today. I . . . as you know, I don't really believe in all that religious stuff. And yet something definitely did happen here today. Something wonderful. Something amazing. I really don't understand it."

"So do you believe now? In God?" Rachel asked.

The doctor smiled. "Let's just say I'm open to the possibility. And I think I'll probably go to church on Sunday. And my husband will say that's a miracle in itself."

"And what about the pregnant lady who'd been hit by the car?"

"She delivered two healthy baby girls."

"Two of them? Amazing." Cooper smiled. "How wonderful."

"They're teeny and they're both in NICU, but according to the doctor they'll both be fine as long as there are no other complications."

After she was gone, Cooper shook his head. "What an amazing day, huh?"

"Unbelievable. It's so . . . so overwhelming to see God work up close like that. I'm in . . . I'm in awe. I have no other word to describe it."

"That's the perfect word, I think. Remember as I was getting ready to leave for Atlanta, and I asked you if you were ready yet. And you said you might not ever be ready."

She laughed. "Yeah, and you said God had a way of making things happen when we least expect it. So, what? You decided to help God out by getting this sick?"

"Not me. I really had no idea I was that sick."

"What did you feel?"

"Just a little achy, and then a lot achy, and

then I don't remember a whole lot after that."

"I've been thinking about what you said. About love."

"Yes."

"And I think you're right. When I tried to heal those other people, I wanted to heal them but I didn't really even care about them. As people. Certainly didn't love them." She sighed. "It never even occurred to me to be concerned about their relationship with God. And that's more important than any physical healing."

He nodded.

She felt the tears welling up. "I feel so awful that I didn't show them God's love. I didn't talk to them about how much God loves them and what He did by sending His only Son down to become our Savior. I really feel horrible. I don't even know if they died without . . ."

"I don't think you should feel bad. I know that's not what God wants from you. Remember Paul tells us to put the past behind us and move forward. It's time for you to move forward."

"You're right." She nodded. "It'll take me a little time to do that. But I'll get there. In the meantime, we have something else to talk about."

"Yes . . ."

She took a deep breath. "If I'm to . . . you know . . . do this healing thing, then I'll need a supernatural love from God for other people." She shrugged. "Mostly because we both know loving others isn't my strong suit."

"I wouldn't say that. You do a great job loving me."

"You make it easy to do that." She patted his cheek. "But I'm talking about love for people as a whole. Even people I don't know. Even people I don't particularly like. Anyway, I know that when I ask for it, if I ask for that supernatural type of love, God will give it to me. And it seems to me that'll change everything."

"What do you mean?"

"I mean if I have this supernatural love for other people, it'll change the way we live."

"How?"

"I'm not exactly sure how. Only that it will. And that it will affect your life as much as mine. I don't have a right to ask you to make that kind of a change."

"That makes perfect sense. Our lives are definitely connected to each other. Like puzzle pieces. Different shapes and colors. Different jobs, but the pieces fit together to finish the puzzle."

She stared. "That's exactly right. Our life — everybody's life is like a jigsaw puzzle. With so many pieces to figure out where they go and how they fit. I want your blessing before I . . . we, go forward with this."

"Oh, dear sweet Rachel. You've had my blessing from the moment you opened your eyes in that hospital room and told me that you had a visit with Jesus."

"It'll mean changes."

He grinned. "Big changes. I knew that the moment you told me Jesus asked if you wanted to be healed or to be a healer. And I'm more than all right with it. Change is a good thing."

"Are you ready for the first one?"

He nodded.

"I want to go home."

"As soon as the doctor releases me."

She shook her head. "I don't mean our house in Cleveland. I mean home."

Cooper smiled. "Oh, that home. Now I understand why we haven't been able to sell it."

The next morning, Dr. Zuchak shook Cooper's hand. "It's been an interesting experience, but now it's time for you to go home."

"Really?"

185

"You have a clean bill of health. I still don't know . . ." She held up a hand. "I know. I know. I'm still having trouble wrapping my brain around it."

Rachel smiled. "Don't worry. God's patient. He'll be there waiting for you when you're ready."

"That's exactly what my husband told me last night."

"He sounds like a smart man."

"He is. The nurse will be here soon with your discharge papers."

"Thanks so much, Dr. Zuchak."

She shrugged. "You're welcome. Even though I'm pretty sure I didn't have anything to do with it."

Raul walked in as the doctor walked out. "Good Morning. Wow, you look a lot better than the last time I saw you, Cooper. You had us plenty scared."

"I'm all better now. Raul, thanks for all you did. Rachel said you were here the whole time."

"I certainly was. And I have to tell you what happened out in the waiting room was miraculous. Wish you could have seen it for yourself."

"I'd have liked to but I was a little busy. In here."

"I've got to tell you, Rachel, when Cooper

told me that God had given you the gift of healing, I was a bit skeptical. But I'm not any longer. I want to help you in any way I can. And I'm not the only one. Every person in the waiting room came up to me. I have their names and addresses for you. They each wanted to thank you. Personally."

"Oh, how sweet. I'll get back to them as soon as we get home. Even though, we'll be sort of busy."

"With what?" Raul asked.

"We've decided to move back home. Then we have to figure out a way for Rachel to use her gift. We've got an idea but it's in the rough stages right now."

"What are you thinking?"

"We're thinking of a retreat. Sort of like a bed and breakfast, but it would be a spiritual retreat where people can come and focus on God and his healing power."

Raul nodded. "That sounds perfect."

"We'll need to think about it some more."

Rachel added, "And pray about it, of course."

"Of course. But it sounds like a great idea. And I'll help make it happen."

The nurse walked in. "I've got your walking papers, Miracle Man. Everyone is talking about what happened."

"Everyone?"

"Oh, yeah, everyone."

"What do you mean?" Rachel asked.

"You'll find out soon enough, my dear." The nurse patted her arm. "I just hope you're ready."

As they left the front entrance of the hospital, a crowd of people stood around. They closed in around Rachel and Cooper. Some held microphones that were shoved at them.

A woman from the crowd yelled out. "Rachel, heal me. Please." That started others yelling the same thing. The people pushed in closer.

Rachel grabbed Cooper's arm and leaned against him. "I didn't expect this."

"Neither did I."

A woman with a microphone pushed through the crowd. "Mrs. Summers, we heard that you healed all the people in the ICU yesterday. Can you tell us what happened? How did you do it? Can you do it again?"

"I didn't heal anyone. Only God heals."

"But —"

Mark Matthews pushed his way through the crowd with a camera crew close behind him. He looked at the other reporter. "This is my story, Anne. Back off. Good to see you again, Rachel."

188

Rachel turned her face from the cameras. She leaned into Cooper. "Please get me out of here."

Cooper held onto her arm as they retreated back inside the hospital.

Mark walked through the double doors talking as he followed them. "But Rachel. I thought you'd be pleased to see me. There are the craziest rumors going around. Everyone's saying —"

"Not now, Mark. My husband's been very sick. We're going home right now." She tugged on Cooper's arm.

Nia laughed as she shook her head. "I guess you got back at him, right? For the bad show he did 'bout you. Making fun of you and everything. Served him right."

Rachel smiled. "That wasn't what it was about at all. I was just shocked by the whole thing. I had no idea they were out there waiting for me. I might have been better prepared if I'd known. I did talk with him eventually, and some of the other reporters. I was big news for a while."

Cooper nodded. "Until something else took hold of their interest."

"Well, I wouldn't of talked to him." Nia shook her finger at Rachel. "You're just too nice. He didn't deserve it."

"I suppose he didn't. But then again, none of us deserve God's love and mercy and He gives it to us freely."

"Like I said. Too nice." Nia looked up from topping the pizzas with cheese. "So you moved down here. To this house?"

"Not quite. But it wasn't too far from here."

"Actually, just a few miles down the road," Cooper said. "Our daughter lives in that house now. With her husband and Jarrod."

On cue, the kitchen door opened. A pretty woman with dark black hair walked in. "Hi, Rachel. Are we too early? Did you have a good trip, Cooper?"

"A great one, honey."

"I'm Janet." She smiled then walked over to hug Rachel. "I wanted to come sooner but Rachel warned me to stay away. She didn't want to be disturbed. Had a special guest she needed to tend to."

Nia looked from Janet to Rachel and then at Cooper. "You're allowed to call them by their first names?"

"Didn't they tell you?"

"Tell me what?"

"I haven't gotten that far in the story yet, Janet."

"Rachel and her stories. Not that they aren't great stories. Rachel's had a very

190

interesting life. Anyway, I'm not their biological daughter."

"You're not?"

"I came to The Puzzle House when I was sixteen, with my Mom, and I never left. Well, I guess technically I did leave since I don't live here. But —"

"So Rachel healed you?"

"In a way. But not the way you mean. We came because my Mom had ALS. Lou Gehrig Disease. Rachel and Cooper opened their house to us and we stayed until my mom died."

"She died. Rachel didn't heal her."

"Only God heals. But yes, God, with Rachel's help, did heal my mother."

"You said she died."

"There are many kinds of healing, Nia. Not just physical healing. And as far as I'm concerned, spiritual healing is much more important than the physical kind." Janet sat down on the stool beside Nia.

"That's easy for you to say. You ain't the one dying."

"Oh, sweetheart. It's not easy for me to say at all. And I'm not discounting anything that you're going through. And I don't want you to die." Janet took her hand. "But I really don't want you to die angry and bitter. That's the way my mother was when we first came here. She was so angry about the ALS. I didn't even know the person she'd become, but Rachel gave me back my mother. The sweet, kind, loving one."

"But she still died."

"She did, but she died at peace. And she's with God now."

Nia bit down on her lip.

Still holding her hand, Janet smiled. "Go ahead. You can tell me what you're thinking. I'm tougher than I look."

A small smile crept on Nia's face. "I ain't got nothing to say. I sort of see what you mean."

"It takes a lot of energy to stay angry all the time. Believe me, I know. It wasn't just my mother who was angry. So was I. As I said, I got healed here, too."

Nia dusted off her hands. "I'm going to lay down for a while. I'm tired."

Jarrod walked in. "Aren't you eating pizza with us? They look great. One thing's for sure. They will taste as great as they look. Grandpa's a great cook."

"I'll be back. Just need to rest for a few minutes."

"Let me help you upstairs." Jarrod held out his arm.

Brandon walked in. "That's OK, Jarrod. I'm going up anyway."

"Where have you been?" Rachel asked.

"Putting the horses away." Brandon smiled. "Did city girl tell you what happened?"

Rachel held up a hand. "Well, what we did discuss was we both want to see you go to Atlanta, get on a bus, make three transfers, and end up at the mall."

"What's a transfer?"

Rachel and Nia looked at each other and started laughing.

"What? What's so funny?"

That made them laugh even harder.

"Come on, city girl. I need to clean up so I don't smell like a horse at dinner."

She held onto Brandon's arm as they walked out of the kitchen.

When the two had left, Janet looked at Rachel. "What? Did I come on too strong?"

"Not at all. I think she just needs a minute or two to herself."

"I didn't mean to chase her away."

"I'm sure she'll come back down in a bit."

Just as the pizzas were being set on the table, Nia walked in. Her eyes were red but she had a smile on her face.

Pizza, laughter, and more stories made the evening go by too quickly.

Before going to bed, Rachel knocked on Nia's door.

"Come in."

Rachel peeked in. "Just wanted to see how you were doing. It's been a big day. Are you feeling OK? Not too tired?"

"I'm a little tired. But it was a good day. It was fun."

Rachel sat on the edge of her bed. "Same here."

Nia giggled. "You know I thought you had this sad and lonely life. Just you in this big house with sick and dying people. Boy was I wrong."

"God has blessed me. I've had a great life, Nia. Filled with more love and joy than I had a right to."

"Yeah, but it's not all been easy."

"That's so very true. Nothing worthwhile . . ."

"Ever is. I sort of get that now. We might not appreciate what we do have if we never had any bad times."

"That's a good way of putting it, Nia."

"And we might not appreciate the good things if we're too focused on the bad things."

"So true."

"So what happened after you moved back here?"

Rachel sighed. "Oh, a lot. I still had my brain tumors to deal with. And the second treatment was even worse than the first. That's when I lost all my hearing in this ear. Not easy at all, but God did use that time to continue to teach me."

"About what?"

"Lots of things. Especially about pain. I mean physical pain. I was never really good at empathy for other people. I was always too busy worrying about myself to think much about anyone else or what they were going through."

"What's empathy?"

"It's being able to put yourself in someone else's shoes and understand what they're going through. Feeling what they're feeling."

"So did you learn to do that?"

"I did, but it wasn't easy. As I said, the second treatment was even more difficult than the first. I was basically housebound for months during that time. But I kept studying the Bible and learning, so it wasn't wasted time. That's when things started coming together for The Puzzle House as well."

"I guess I've been wasting a lot of time being angry and feeling sorry for myself. Or like Brandon says, having a pity party. God must be pretty mad at me."

"Not at all. God loves you. Very much."

Rachel placed a hand on her arm. Nia leaned in a little closer. Rachel put her arms around the young girl's shoulders. "I am so sorry this is happening to you."

Tears welled up in Nia's eyes. "Me, too."

She laid her head on Rachel's shoulders and sobbed. Rachel rocked her and told her how much God loved her. When the storm subsided, Nia moved away from her. "I'm . . . I'm sorry."

Rachel straightened up, ignoring the fact her back hurt from the awkward position. "For what, Nia? It's OK to be sad or angry or both. Or whatever you're feeling. You're in a difficult situation. And besides God can take it. As Annie said, He's tough."

A small smile played on Nia's lips. "If you say so. "So you started healing people after that?"

"Not me. God."

"Cause you're just the cord, right?"

"Right."

"And I have to be the one to turn on the light."

"Right again."

"With my faith." She looked at Rachel, tears in her eyes. "But I don't think I have any faith."

"Romans 12:3 tell us that God gives each of us a portion of faith. So it's there, but we have to learn how to use it."

"But how do I turn on that switch?"

Rachel squeezed Nia's hand. "I think you just did. Would you like me to pray with you now?"

12

The next morning Rachel stared out the window of The Puzzle Room, enjoying the beautiful sunrise. Just enough light to brighten up the fall colors of the trees. The early morning colors shimmered across the lake.

An amazing sight, but not more amazing than the sight of Nia sitting on her bed with tears streaming down her cheeks as they prayed. As she accepted Jesus as her Savior. That was pure beauty.

Would God heal Nia? As Janet had said last night, there was more than one type of healing. Physically, Rachel thought God would give Nia her miracle, but Nia's spiritual healing had already begun.

From where Rachel sat she couldn't see Cooper, but he was out there taking pictures with the hope that one of them would make a perfect puzzle for someone. Many of the puzzles came from Cooper's camera. Others were from Janet, who had a gift of drawing. Some even came from past guests as well. Brandon had contributed a few. The ones with stick people and tilted houses, from some of the younger guests, were among Rachel's favorites.

Nia opened her eyes. Had Rachel — no God — had God healed her? If the answer was no, she didn't want to know. She was afraid to move, not wanting to feel the too familiar tiredness. And achiness as if she was just getting the flu.

Staring up at the ceiling, she imagined what it would be like if she stood up and instead of feeling so tired she could barely walk, she'd run down the steps. If she stood up, and there was no pain. If. But she couldn't lie in bed all day pretending.

Looking at the sun streaming into her window, she might have spent a lot of the day in bed already. Most mornings it was still dark when she woke up.

One thing was for sure, she'd slept better last night than she had in a long time. But that might have been because she'd stayed up so late. She and Rachel had spent a long time praying last night. Then talking. Then praying some more.

There'd been no warmth, no tingling, as

Rachel held her hand and prayed — no begged — for God to heal Nia. But Rachel explained that it didn't always happen that way.

Jesus's miracles in the Bible were different each time. Sometimes people were healed instantly. Other times, it was gradual. And still other times, it didn't happen. At all. Would this be one of those times?

She sighed.

Time to find out.

Nia sat up. Tears filled her eyes. The pain was still there. It hadn't worked. She wasn't any better than she'd been yesterday. God hadn't healed her. Curling into a ball, Nia swiped at the tears making their way down her cheeks. Why would He care about her? She was a nobody. She was . . .

Not true, my dear sweet Nia. Rachel's voice spoke softly in her head, almost as if she were in the room with her. She'd told Nia over and over last night. *You are a child of God, well-loved and powerful. Never forget powerful. You can be pitiful or powerful, but you can't be both.*

Nia's gaze fell on the lamp on her nightstand.

Faith. Rachel had told her that faith is believing without seeing. Well she wasn't seeing any difference, but she could still

200

believe. "Gotta have faith. Faith produces miracles. And I want a miracle." She reached over and turned on the light. "God, I believe you're healing me. Even if I can't see it. Or feel it." She felt silly talking to an empty room but Rachel had told her it was important to say words of faith out loud. So she did. "I'm getting healthier. Stronger. My cancer is dying. And . . . and I'm going to live. Because You love me."

When she wheeled herself into the Puzzle Room, Rachel and Brandon were at his table. He waved. "I just finished my puzzle."

"Good for you, country boy."

He motioned for her. "Come see it. It's pretty cool."

She maneuvered the wheelchair between the tables.

"Are you OK?" Brandon asked.

"A little tired. I think I stayed up too late talking with Rachel." She looked at Brandon's puzzle. It was one of the old-fashioned paintings. It showed two men, one with a beard and one that was naked. Their hands were stretched out to each other but not quite touching.

"It's called The Creation of Adam. By Michelangelo. It's part of a painting on the ceiling of the Sistine Chapel." Brandon told her. "It's a very famous painting."

"Indeed it is," Rachel said. "God is reaching His hand towards Adam. And that's what He does for each of us, He wants to be a part of our lives but in the end, we're the ones who make that decision by bridging the gap."

"I saw this painting at the Sistine Chapel. How cool is that? I can't believe that's what my puzzle ended up being this time. This is definitely the best puzzle I've done so far. It tells me that God's right beside me. He's always there watching over me. Protecting me." Brandon gave a delighted grin.

Nia stared at the puzzle, and then gazed at Brandon. Her stomach twisted. That wasn't what it was telling her. It was almost as if God was reaching for Brandon like . . . she tore her gaze away from it. "Well, my puzzle's a mess. Maybe you should help me with it or I'll never get it finished."

"Can't do that. Only you and Rachel work on a puzzle together."

"A lot of good you are, country boy." She wheeled to her own puzzle table, grateful she didn't have to walk.

Rachel and Brandon whispered to each other.

"Hey, city girl. Still want to ride that horse?"

She was too tired to do anything.

Brandon was smiling at her.

"Sure."

"OK, I'll be back later. We'll go after lunch." He left.

Rachel came to her table.

"What do you think Brandon's puzzle means?" Nia asked.

A sad expression crossed Rachel's face.

"Yea, that's what I thought, too. It almost looked as if God was getting ready to yank country boy up. Is . . . is Brandon sick? I thought he was just here to help you and your sick guests. He looks healthy enough. Seems to be all right to me."

"Only on the outside. He has some heart issues. That's one of the reasons he keeps leaving. It's important for him to rest frequently."

"Is he getting better?"

Rachel met her gaze with unshed tears in her eyes.

"But . . ." Nia had no idea how to finish her sentence.

Rachel patted her hand. "It's OK. Brandon is at peace with God. And himself."

"He seems so happy. Not sad or angry like me."

"He's had a lot of time to get used to the idea. He's been sick for a long time."

Shame filled her. Brandon had been nice

to her since the moment she got here. And he was just as sick as her. "I guess he was talking about himself when he said no pity parties allowed."

"Most assuredly, he was."

They both worked on the puzzle for a few minutes. "I see you aren't feeling any better today."

"Pretty tired."

"That's not surprising since you had a busy day yesterday, but it was probably a big disappointment for you."

"Sorta. But I did like you told me. I talked to God and told him I was still believing I was getting healthier by the minute. And that I'm waiting for His miracle."

"Good for you."

Nia stared out the window, and then looked back at Rachel. "Even this city girl can admit that's a pretty awesome view. No wonder you like living here. You get to see that every morning."

"I'm very blessed. But it's even more special today because you're here to share it with me."

"Yeah you keep telling me how special I am."

"Do you believe me?"

Nia grinned. "I'm starting to. But I don't understand why."

Rachel grinned. "Are you sure you don't have even a little inkling of why that is?"

"Not a clue."

"Well, think back to when your aunt dropped you off, and you might just figure it out."

"Why don't you just tell me?"

"It's more fun this way. There's nothing like a good mystery in books, and some-times, in life."

"I know it's up to God and everything, but do you think I got healed last night, Rachel? I kind of thought that happened when we prayed. I didn't think I'd need the wheelchair today."

"Sometimes people get healed in a mirac-ulously instant way, but not very often." Rachel adjusted so she was facing Nia. "And remember there are different kinds of heal-ing. Physical healing is one, but it's not the most important kind."

"Like what Janet said."

"Exactly. I can't tell you about the physi-cal healing part even though I know that's the kind we prayed for last night. But the spiritual healing? I can give you a pretty definite yes on that one."

"Why?"

Rachel reached up and touched Nia's cheek. "Because of the beautiful smile on your face this morning. That wasn't there yesterday or the day you came here."

Nia laughed. "Yeah, I guess I was sort of mad and unhappy. I'm sorry I wasn't nicer to you."

"And how do you feel now?"

"Hopeful and loved. By God and by you and Auntie and all my friends."

"And let's not forget about faith."

"Let's not."

"Faith is so important, Nia. Our faith allows God to work in our life. The important thing to know in the coming days is that your faith and hope and even the love might be tested. You need to pass the test."

"How?"

"By not giving up. By believing God loves you no matter what is happening to you. And that happens by studying the Bible. An attitude of gratitude works for me. Praising God for what I do have. Focusing on the good in my life, not the bad."

"That don't sound all that easy to do."

"So true. It can be downright difficult. But that's when it's the most important. Faith isn't about a moment. It's about a lifetime of moments. Especially when you don't see or get what you want. That's when the devil tries to take advantage. He tries to tell you God isn't there. That He's not real.

That He doesn't love you."

"Like me having to use my wheelchair this morning?"

"Exactly. And every time that devils whispers in your ear that God doesn't love you, that God can't heal you; that's when you've got to yell right back at him that God does love you and that God's way is the best way. Even when we don't understand it."

"And I sure don't understand it. It's so confusing. Sort of like my puzzle was at first."

"And then it wasn't as confusing as the week went on."

Cooper walked in carrying a plate. "Cookies for my two favorite cookies."

"That's so lame, Cooper," Nia said.

"Really? Because I thought it was quite clever." He sighed theatrically as he set the plate on the puzzle table. "Oh, well, I'll let you have a cookie anyway even if you don't appreciate my humor."

"Wow. I hope it tastes as good as it smells." Nia grinned at him.

"Try it."

She broke the cookie in half and popped it in her mouth. Her thumbs up was her answer.

"Cooper's cookies are spectacular," Rachel said as she picked one up. "I will leave you to your puzzle, but when Brandon's ready to take you for the horse ride, come get me. I'll be in my room."

"Will do."

Cooper and Rachel walked out of the room, holding hands.

Brandon gave Nia's wheelchair a shove, and then she was in the barn.

"Eww. It's smelly in here."

"What do you expect, city girl? It's a barn."

Rachel walked in right behind them, laughing as she went over to Mindy's stall. The horse put her head against Rachel's. "Hi, girl. Sorry I haven't been down to see you in a while."

The horse whinnied and rubbed her head against Rachel's palm.

"Yes, I have what you're looking for." She reached into her pocket and held out a slice of apple.

The horse whinnied again, bared her teeth, and moved closer to Rachel's hand.

"She's gonna bite you," Nia squealed.

"You really are such a city girl," Brandon said.

"And I do not take that as an insult, country boy. I love being a city girl. Nothing wrong with it. So there."

"You ready to get on the horse?" Rachel asked.

Nia looked at the huge animal. "I guess. If you say it's safe, then I trust you."

"It's safe." Rachel smiled. "You're my special girl, so I wouldn't let anything happen to you."

Cooper walked in. "I thought you could use a little help getting Nia up there."

"Oh, sure. You just wanted to see me make a fool of myself too."

"No comment."

"Everyone wanting to watch the city girl fall off the horse."

Brandon led the horse out its stall, and put on the saddle and other gear.

Cooper carried over a foot stool. "OK, Nia. You get on the stool, and then I'll hoist you on the horse. He might move a little but he'll not bolt away. I promise."

"And then I'll lead the horse for you. So all you have to do is hold on and enjoy the ride." Brandon played with the reins.

"You aren't riding?"

"Not this time. I want you to enjoy your first horse experience. To not be afraid that you'll do something wrong. So I'm going to take care of you."

All of them were going out of their way for her. And she hadn't done anything for any of them. Overcome with emotion, she looked down at the floor of the stable to get her feelings under control. She lifted her head with a smile. "Let's do this."

Brandon guided her out of the barn.

Rachel and Cooper walked in front of them.

Rachel waved at them as she and Cooper veered back toward the house. "Have fun."

They walked away holding hands.

"They sure seem to love each other, don't they?"

Brandon patted the horses shoulder. "They do. That's the kind of marriage I'd want. If I had one. Which I probably won't."

She decided to act as if she didn't know. "Why not? Don't you want to get married?"

"Sure, I'd love to, but even if I lived long enough to get married, it wouldn't be fair to my wife. Sooner or later, she'd be alone."

"I wonder if Rachel ever felt that way. With Cooper. She's had brain tumors for a long time now. And it doesn't seem to have made a difference to them. They still love each other."

"That's true."

"What do you mean if you live long enough?" Nia's courage almost failed her.

He grinned. "It's OK. Rachel told me that she'd told you about my heart condition."

"Oh."

His hand was still on the horse's shoulder so she leaned down and put her hand over his. "I'm really sorry."

"It's OK. I actually thought I'd die a long time ago. So anything after that is bonus time. And I've got to do a lot more than I ever thought I would."

"Like what?"

"My parents have taken me to Alaska and Europe. I got to see the Rocky Mountains and the Pacific Ocean. And lots more. But more important than my trips was getting to know God. That's why I'm not afraid."

"Oh."

"Well, I'm a little afraid but . . ." He shrugged. "But no pity parties allowed."

She straightened up and took her hand away. "You don't seem afraid. You seem so brave."

He laughed. " 'Course there is one thing I still need to do."

"What's that?"

"My secret."

"Come on, country boy. Tell me."

"Nah, you'll just make fun of me, city girl."

"I won't. I promise. Now tell me."

"I was hoping to fall in love. At least a little."

"Yeah me too, country boy, me too."

They went around the pond and then made their way back to the barn.

Brandon walked to the side of the horse and held up his arms. "OK, slide off. I won't let you fall."

"I trust you." She wasn't sure that was true, but she said it anyway. His smile told her it had been the right thing to say. She swung a leg over and then moved closer. His arms held her steady as she slid off the horse. And then they were face to face, his arms still around her. Neither of them moved.

His hand reached up and brushed her cheek.

She smiled.

"I'm thinking I'd like to kiss you."

"I'm thinking that's a good idea."

He leaned in and their lips met.

When they parted, they both had silly smiles.

Nia felt shy, almost embarrassed. "I . . . I . . . that was my first kiss."

"Really?"

"Really." She bumped her shoulder into his. "It was nice."

"Nice? That's all you've got to say. Nice."

She laughed. "Really nice."

"That's better." He moved in and kissed

her again.

"OK, country boy. We better get to the house."

"Sounds like a good idea. Of course staying here with you might be a better idea."

"I don't think so."

He held her hand as they walked out of the barn. "I can't believe how lucky I am. I got to kiss the most beautiful girl in the world."

"Beautiful? You better get your eyes checked, country boy. There ain't nothing beautiful about this bald head or this skinny body."

"You're so wrong about that. You're very beautiful." He leaned in and kissed her cheek again.

13

Nia opened her eyes and smiled as she thought about Brandon. He really was so nice. Maybe God would heal him. Even if Rachel didn't think so. She'd already said God didn't always keep her in the loop.

She closed her eyes and prayed that Brandon would be healed. They probably wouldn't ever see each other again after they left here, but she still wanted him to live a long and happy life and to fall in love. Or maybe they would see each other again?

She grinned as fantasies played out in her head. Going to the prom. Together. College. Together. And a wedding with Cooper escorting her down the aisle. With her handsome groom waiting for her. Brandon.

Silly, she knew. They were both way too young for such a commitment. But that didn't mean it couldn't happen. Later. For now their friendship was enough. Her finger outlined her lips. And maybe a few kisses now and then.

"Earth to Nia," she muttered. Enough daydreaming. Time to face the day. She only had a few more days left at The Puzzle House and she was determined to finish her puzzle.

After showering and dressing, she walked to her door. A piece of paper lay in front of it. She picked it up and then smiled. A note from Brandon.

Hey City Girl, here's the words to my song. See if you can fix it up and put a new melody with it. Make it your own. I know it will be awesome! Your Country Boy.

She'd do that later. With a smile she left her room. The quiet was noticeable. Usually, people were up and moving. No one was in the Puzzle Room so she went to the kitchen. No Cooper. She shivered. It was way too quiet.

Where was everyone?

After eating a simple breakfast of toast and juice, she sat down and worked on her puzzle. An hour went by and still no one. It was an unspoken rule that everyone was allowed to sleep as long as they wanted but the quiet was creeping her out.

Rachel and Cooper wouldn't mind if she knocked on their door. At the bottom of the steps, she stared at the lift. Nah, she could walk the steps. It was quicker anyway.

When she was at the top, she took a few deep breaths. And felt a sense of accomplishment. It was the first time she'd walked them. When she knocked on Rachel and Cooper's door, no one answered.

She moved to Brandon's door with the same results. Maybe they all went out for an early horseback ride.

Without the newbie to slow them down.

Oh, well. Might as well do something. She picked up Brandon's lyrics and made her way back to the Puzzle Room, and her guitar. Another hour went by as she strummed and changed the words around and strummed again.

A car drove in.

Rachel and Cooper were walking up the steps just as she opened the door. Cooper held on to Rachel's elbow as they both looked at her with puffy, red eyes.

Her mind wouldn't work and she couldn't breathe.

Rachel put her arms around Nia. "I'm sorry, my sweet Nia."

"What? What's wrong?"

"Brandon's gone."

"He wouldn't leave without saying goodbye to me. He said his Dad was picking him up later. Not this early. He wouldn't just leave." She could hear the begging in her voice.

Rachel stepped back. Her voice was soft. "That's not what I meant, Nia. He didn't go home with his parents. He went home to God."

Nia backed away. "That's not true. You're lying. He was fine yesterday."

Cooper put his hand on her shoulder. "It was a shock to us, as well."

She didn't want to hear this. Not any of it. "It's not fair. Why would God do that to him?" To her. She ran up the steps, but stumbled half-way up. Sprawled on the steps, she cried.

A moment later Rachel's arm touched her back. "It's OK, sweetie. Be as sad and angry as you want. For us. But don't be sad for Brandon. He's with God. And that's a wonderful thing."

Nia sobbed while Rachel rubbed her back. Finally the tears stopped. She rolled on her back and sat up. "I . . . I can't believe this. I knew you said he was sick but I didn't know he was that sick."

"That's because Brandon didn't want you to know. He simply enjoyed each day that God chose to give him. Without the pity party."

Nia wiped at her eyes. "He did hate the

pity parties."

Rachel's arms went around her and Nia leaned closer. They sat that way for a long time.

Finally, Nia asked, "What happened?"

"He slept with an oxygen mask and a monitor. The monitor receiver was in our room. In the middle of the night, its alarm woke us. When we checked on him, he was already . . . at peace."

Nia put her head on her knees and sobbed some more. "I wish you could have healed him."

"God had other plans. And Brandon knew that. I know this is hard. But you know what Brandon would say, right?"

Through her tears, she looked at Rachel. "No pity party."

"Exactly. Uh, I happened to notice you ran up the steps."

"and . . . and I walked up a while ago when I was looking for you. I didn't even think about that when I did it. And . . . nothing's hurting on me either."

Rachel patted her hand. "God is so good."

"But —"

"His ways are not our ways, my dear sweet Nia."

Nia nodded then stood up. "You're right. God is so good."

"Where are you going?"
"I have a song to finish."

14

It was a picture perfect day.

Just the kind of day Brandon would love. Chairs had been set up so that the mourners had a view of the pond as they looked at each speaker. The pond that Brandon loved so much.

Nia never did get around to going fishing with him. So much they wouldn't get to do together, now. But he had taken her on her first horse ride. And he'd been the first to kiss her.

She touched her lips, still feeling the sweet warmth of his lips against hers. She remembered his words about wanting to fall in love — at least a little. She smiled. God had given him that, too.

Cooper finished praying, and then his gaze met hers.

Nodding, Nia stood and made her way to the front with her guitar. *Help me do this, God.* She turned and faced the group. "I didn't know Brandon as long as the rest of you. But, oh, the time we shared was so special to me. And I like to think to him, too."

Nia looked at Brandon's mother in the front row. Tears streamed down her cheeks but she was smiling.

Nia held up her guitar. "Brandon gave me this. And then we both spent time playing it and singing together. Brandon wrote a song and then he gave it to me. Told me to fix it. And make it my own. I tried, but the truth is, it's Brandon's song and it was perfect just the way he wrote it. I'd like to sing it for you."

Darkness and trouble
No joy
No peace to be found.
Only sickness and sorrow abound.
No one around but . . .

The God of Creation never forsakes.
He is the God of Abraham, Isaac, and
   Jacob.
He is my God
And He is so good.
His love endures forever and a day.

He is . . . Jehova Rapha

The Lord who heals.
The Lord who heals.

And nothing is impossible.
No nothing is impossible for my God.
His love endures forever and a day.

He is . . . Jehova Rapha
The Lord who heals.
The Lord who heals.

He changes the darkness to light.
His peace brings joy and delight.
He is with us day and night.
His love endures forever and a day.

His promises are real.
His promises are true.
And He will never leave.
His love endures forever and a day.

My God is . . . Jehova Rapha
The Lord who heals.
The Lord who heals.
His love endures forever and a day.

He is . . . Jehova Rapha
The Lord who heals.
The Lord who heals.
His love endures forever and a day.

15

Nia walked into the Puzzle Room. A new puzzle was on the wall. Brandon's puzzle. She walked over and stared at God reaching for Adam. There was a picture of Brandon below it, holding a fish and looking happy.

Rachel walked up behind her. "There's a verse in the Bible that says draw near to God and He will draw near to you. Never forget that, Nia. God lets you be in control of your relationship with Him. He's always there, waiting and hoping. But it's up to you."

Nia nodded. "Do you think Brandon knew what his puzzle meant?"

"I think a puzzle can mean many things. And I think Brandon was right when he said it meant that God was with him always. But, yes, I think he also knew it wouldn't be too long before his fingers would touch God's."

"I like that. That's a nice way of thinking

about it." She thought of how nice it felt when Brandon had held her hand. "It must be amazing to hold hands with Jesus."

Rachel grinned. "You have no idea."

"Oh, yeah. I almost forgot you got to do that, too."

"It changes everything."

"Speaking of puzzles, I gotta finish mine before Auntie comes to pick me up." Her glance lingered on Brandon's picture, and then she walked to the puzzle table. "I just want to thank you for . . . for helping me with my puzzle."

"My pleasure. Cooper's out snapping pictures this morning so what would you like for breakfast?"

"One of your toasted cheese sandwiches."

"Coming up."

Rachel stared at a burnt cheese sandwich. Was it savable? Probably. Edible? She wasn't so sure about that. She nibbled at the edge of it and grimaced. Maybe it was edible, but not to her, and she wouldn't even think of subjecting Nia to it. She tossed it in the sink. The garbage disposal could make a nice breakfast of it.

Someone screamed.

She grabbed her cane and hurried to the Puzzle Room.

Nia was sitting there, glaring at her. "It's not fair."

"What's that, my dear?"

"I did all this work. It's finished."

"That's a good thing."

"It's not a good thing. There's a piece missing." Her finger slammed down on the card table where the missing puzzle piece was.

"Oh, dear, really?"

"I did all this work and now I can't even finish it. It's not fair."

"But you should feel good about that. You finished. Sure a piece might be missing, but so what? You —"

"So what? So what? So I wouldn't have worked this hard if I'd known this would happen."

"I understand what you mean." Rachel nodded. "It's really frustrating when we work hard, do the right things, and life still doesn't turn out the way we expect or want it to."

Nia gave her an assessing glance. "Is that what this is about? Did you take my puzzle piece when I wasn't looking?"

"Is what what's about?"

"Another puzzle lesson."

"I promise you I did not take your puzzle piece. But do you think there's something to be learned here?"

Nia rolled her eyes. "I suppose I shouldn't let little things like one little missing puzzle piece bother me that much."

"Sounds right to me."

"And I suppose you're right. I did the best I could. I should be proud of that, I guess. It's not my fault a piece is missing." She tapped the table. "Sometimes life just happens."

"That's for sure. We can't always control our circumstances but we can always control our reactions to them. And we should always choose to act in a way that will make God smile."

Nia sighed.

"I need to go out and make us some more toasted cheese sandwiches. The first ones didn't turn out so well. I burned them."

Nia laughed. "I guess it's just like you said, life doesn't always turn out the way we expect it to."

"That's for sure, my dear, especially when I'm the one doing the cooking."

Rachel touched the completed puzzle. "Notice how the pieces interlock. Each piece needs the other. Without one of the pieces, the picture's not complete." She touched the spot where the piece was missing.

"I can see that. That's why I'm aggravated."

"I told you about what happened in the hospital when Cooper was so sick. But there's a little more to the story that I want you to hear." She sat down.

"Good. It might take my mind off that missing piece."

"Every one of the people who were healed in the ICU that day played a part in my puzzle." Her arm waved around the room. "This puzzle. Without them, The Puzzle House wouldn't exist."

"Really?"

"I believe God put each of them in that room for a reason."

"Really?"

"Well, for example. The young man with the colon cancer. His name is Daniel Landers."

"The Daniel Landers?"

"Oh, so you've heard of him?"

"Everyone has. He's so rich."

"Daniel's been very generous. He helped us obtain this property. And built my beautiful home."

"Wow."

"He's the reason why people don't have to pay when they come to The Puzzle House. And then the young girl with the mother in the car accident."

"What'd she do?"

"She's a very talented artist. She created the first puzzles we used here and many more since then."

"Cool. And what about the pregnant woman?"

"Well, she had those two beautiful twin girls."

"So she didn't do nothing for you."

"I didn't say that."

Nia opened her mouth but stopped before she actually said anything. Then she shook her head. Her fingers ran across the puzzle. Nia swallowed hard. "What date was it when you healed all those people?"

"Now that is an interesting question, my dear, sweet Nia. Why would you ask that?"

Nia sat at the table with a smile. "I think I just figured out why you keep saying I'm so special."

"Really? Well, let's hear your theory."

"Was it May 12?"

"It was."

"That's the day my mom and my auntie were born. In Atlanta. I think that means my grandma was the pregnant lady who pushed that girl out of the way so the car didn't hit her."

"I think you are exactly right."

"You saved my Grandmother that day, and my auntie and my mom?"

"Only God saves, my dear."

"But it was you. If you hadn't been there that day, I would never of been born." Nia wiped away tears.

"God does have an amazing way of working things out just the way they were meant to be." Rachel wiped away her own tears as she put her arms around Nia. "And now you know why you are so precious to me."

"I can't believe it. God really is so amazing."

"He is. That's how life is." Rachel ran her hand across the puzzle. "We don't always get to know how each piece fits into our puzzle at the time we want to know. But God always works it out for our good."

"It's just so hard, sometimes."

"Yes, it is. And when it gets too hard, think of Mary and Joseph and how difficult things were for them. I should go make us those sandwiches. Again."

"Not to be mean, but you really aren't much of a cook. No offense."

"None taken my dear, but we still need to eat. Ten minutes." Using her cane, she walked to the door.

"Hey Rachel, I just thought of something."

Rachel smiled as she turned back. "Really?

What's that?"

"You told me there's no giving up at The Puzzle House. If there's no giving up, then there's no giving up."

"I did tell you that."

"I'll look for that last piece."

"Splendid idea. I'll let you know when lunch is ready." Fifteen minutes later, Rachel walked back in the room.

Nia was sitting in her chair with a big smile holding the missing puzzle piece. "I found it."

"So you did. Where was it?"

"Under the couch. It probably landed there when I knocked the puzzle pieces off the table. I was such a brat, then."

"No comment, my dear, sweet Nia."

"I was waiting until you got here before I put the last piece of the puzzle in."

"I'm honored."

Nia rolled her eyes. "It's not that big of a deal. It's just a puzzle."

"It's not just a puzzle. It's your puzzle."

Nia put her arms around Rachel. "Thank you, Rachel, for helping with my puzzle."

"It was my pleasure. Now let me get my camera." She got it and aimed the camera. "OK. Let's finish this puzzle." As Nia placed the final piece, Rachel snapped several pictures.

"Woo-hoo!" Nia held up her hands as if she'd won a marathon. And maybe she had. "So what now?"

"Now Cooper puts on some kind of magic glue that holds the puzzle together and we display it on the wall with all the others. I'll put yours right beside Brandon's."

"I'd like that." Nia stared at the puzzle, and then looked at Rachel. "You said that lots of the puzzles have special meaning for the person who put it together, so what's this one mean?"

A mixture of dark and light clouds surrounded The Puzzle House. In the middle of the dark clouds right behind the house, the sun shone through, spectacularly creating an amazing rainbow.

"I remember the day Cooper took that picture. There'd been a violent storm only minutes before. We thought there might be a rainbow so we hurried out. And that's what we saw."

"It's just beautiful."

Rachel stared at the finished puzzle, knowing she'd been right about Nia, and where she fit into Rachel's puzzle. "All our puzzles are beautiful, my dear, sweet Nia."

"But you didn't tell me what it means?"

"That's up to you to figure out, my dear,

sweet Nia. It's part of the fun of doing a puzzle."

16

"Slow down."

"If I slow down any more, Auntie, the car won't be moving."

"I don't care. Slow down some more. You haven't had enough experience driving to know what to do with slippery roads."

Nia took her foot off the gas a little. The car slowed. "There, are you happy?"

"I shouldn't have let you drive."

"We still alive, ain't we?" She looked over at her aunt.

"Keep your eyes on the road. You know what? Just pull over so I can drive the rest of the way. I had no idea we were driving into a storm."

Nia turned her focus back on the road. "We're almost there."

"It can't be a second too soon for me."

"Or me." It had been four months since her time at The Puzzle House. It was hard to put into words how different her life was now from the first time they'd made the drive.

Her life. Even if this life was shorter than what Nia would choose, it was OK. Because Nia knew there was another life waiting for her. A better life. One free from pain and sickness. And Brandon would be there. But she didn't think that would happen anytime soon.

Instead, she had hope of a life now. A real life. Thanks to Rachel. And to God, of course. But without Rachel she wouldn't know God the way she did now. Or understand just how awesome He was. She looked over at her aunt. "You don't think she's mad at me, do you? That she'll take back my healing."

"Nia Johnson, that is one of the most ridiculous things I've ever heard you say." Margaretta laughed. "And I've heard you say some pretty ridiculous things."

Nia giggled. "I suppose it is. Rachel would never do something like that. She's just too nice. I can't believe I didn't want to come here. What a dummy I was back then."

"I prefer the word stubborn."

"Yeah, whatevs." She grinned, and then it disappeared. "But I wonder what she wants. It sounded important when she called."

"I guess you'll find out soon enough."

They pulled into the drive. Instead of the fall colors, she was greeted with brown barren trees mixed in among the still green pines. Winter had come to the Georgia mountains.

Nia shut off the car and then looked at Auntie. "Aren't you coming?"

Her aunt waved a hand. "I'll be there in a minute. First I need to breathe for a while, and then I might stretch my legs since the rain stopped."

"It wasn't that bad, Auntie."

"I know. It's not you, it's me." Margaretta smiled, but it didn't quite reach her eyes.

"Go on, now. She's waiting for you."

Nia took a deep breath as she stepped out of the car. No wheelchair this time. Every day, she grew a bit stronger. The doctors hadn't said the word remission. Yet. But they would soon, she was sure of it.

But Nia had a secret. It wasn't remission. God had healed her in his loving goodness. And now that he had, Nia would use her time here on earth to help others. She wasn't quite sure how, but she was young. There was time to figure it out.

Nia had so much to tell Rachel about the last few months. About all she'd been learning as she studied the Bible. Who knew something that old could be so useful today?

Of course, they'd talked on the phone several times. But in person was different. Better.

Nia stared, unable to take another step.

The sun had broken through the dark clouds. A small rainbow was right above The Puzzle House. Like in her puzzle. In fact, it was almost identical to her puzzle. Butterflies swirled in her stomach. What was that about? A few moments before she'd been excited about seeing Rachel, but now something felt . . . wrong.

As her feet hit the first step the door opened. "Hey, Jarrod." His eyes were red. He smiled but his heart didn't seem in it. "I'm glad you made it in time."

"In time?" More foreboding. "For what?"

"Grandma's upstairs. She's waiting for you."

"Why is she upstairs? Is she sick?"

"She'll explain everything to you." He looked at her. "You look like you're feeling better."

"Much better."

Jarrod held the door open for her.

Her gaze went to the Bible verse, just as they had the first time she'd walked into the house. She stared up at the sign with a smile.

WELCOME TO THE PUZZLE HOUSE

And now these three remain: faith, hope and love. But the greatest of these is love.

Rachel had taught her so much about all three of them. And about life. And God. Who would have ever thought an old white lady could teach her anything? And change her life so much?

God really was amazing.

"Is everything all right?" Nia asked, swinging back to Jarrod.

"Hey, would you like to see your puzzle before you go up?" He tugged her arm toward the Puzzle Room.

"I guess so, since it don't seem like I have a choice."

"You know what Grandma always says."

"We always have a choice."

In the Puzzle Room, several people sat on the sofa and chairs. They said nothing. She felt the butterflies again. Something was going on. She was sure of it.

Jarrod led her to a spot in the middle of the wall. There hung her puzzle right beside Brandon's.

Dear, sweet Brandon. She missed him so much. Her hand touched his picture. She would have liked to have had more time with him. She turned back to her own puzzle. Nia ran her fingers across it, feeling the slight bumps from the puzzle pieces. She shivered. It was weird how much that puzzle looked like the scene she'd just seen outside. Except that it looked more like summer than winter.

Jarrod touched the rainbow. "You know rainbows signify God's promises, right?"

"To not destroy the earth with another flood."

"True, but I think it's more than just a promise about that. Grandma says it's a promise He will love us always. And that even though we have rain, there's beauty that comes from the rain."

Nia thought of the storms she'd already weathered in her life. "I like that. I was a little surprised that my puzzle turned out to be a picture of The Puzzle House. What do you think it means?"

He smiled at her. "What do you think it means?"

"You're just like your grandma. I don't know. I've seen The Puzzle House in the summer and now the winter. So, I'm guessing this means I'll be seeing it this spring."

"Could be. Grandma's waiting for you. You better go on up."

"Aren't you coming?"

"She wants to talk with you alone."

With each step, her reluctance grew. As she approached Rachel's room, Nia took a deep breath then knocked.

The door opened.

"Oh, Nia. I'm so glad you're here." Cooper's arms went around her. "I . . . well. I'll let Rachel talk with you first. I'll be back in a few minutes."

Rachel was lying in bed, her eyes were closed. She didn't look well. She opened her eyes. "Oh, Nia. It's so nice to see you. Come sit with me, sweetie." Her voice was soft. Weak.

"What's wrong, Rachel? Are you sick?"

"I believe my puzzle's about to be finished."

As the meaning of Rachel's words hit her, Nia shook her head and backed away from the bed. "No, no, no. That's not true. You don't mean that. God wouldn't do that to you."

"Everybody dies, Nia. It's a part of life."

"But you can't. I need you. Everybody needs you."

"It's not me you need. It's God. We all need God. Remember that always. God will see you through whatever happens in your life. The good times and the bad."

"But I . . . I love you."

"And I love you, my dear, sweet Nia.

That's why I wanted to talk to you before I go." Rachel reached for her hand.

Nia reached out for her. When their hands met, Nia felt warmth, a calming peace.

Rachel pulled her to the bed. "Sit with me. I need to tell you something."

Nia sat down. "What's wrong with you? I just don't . . . can't the doctors do something? And what about God?"

"God has been so good to me. I've had a wonderful life. More than I ever deserved. And I'm ready to see Jesus again. It's been way too long since I saw his beautiful face."

"No, you have to fight it, Rachel. Have faith that you can get better. That's what you taught me. Now, I'm telling you. You gotta have faith, hope, and love."

"I do, my sweet Nia. Faith that I'll be in heaven soon. Hope that the Father will tell me, 'Well done my good and faithful servant.' And love. Oh, so much love. I can't even express it in words."

"But what about Cooper? He loves you so much. He won't —"

"He does love me, but he'll be OK. Because of his own faith. I didn't take this journey alone. We've been in it together from the start. And you'll be here to help him with his sadness."

"Me?"

"You."

"What do you mean?"

"Do you remember how I told you that you were special?"

Nia nodded, unable to speak past the lump in her throat.

"And you said I probably told everyone that. And you were right I do. But I always knew you were different. More special. At least to me."

"Because . . . I was going to be your last . . . the last person you healed. And if you hadn't been in the hospital that day, my mom and my auntie might not have lived and then I never would have been born."

"Again, that was God. I was just the cord. I had a suspicion about you from the moment your aunt contacted me. And then when I saw your finished puzzle, I knew I was right."

"Right about what?

"Nia. Do you know what your name means?"

She shook her head.

"In Swahili your name means purpose."

"I didn't know that."

"Nia, I believe you have a great purpose in this life. God saved your mother and auntie and grandmother for a purpose. So you could be born. And then you got sick for a purpose. To bring you here. To The Puzzle House. So we could spend time together. So you could come to know God more fully."

"Why?"

"Each of us has a purpose in this life. When God creates us, His touch lingers for just a moment or two. In that touch, he gives us talents and passions. That is His gift to each of us. Our gift to Him is to use them to honor Him."

"Like you have."

"Like I've tried to do. I believe you have a purpose. Here at The Puzzle House."

"Here?"

"It's why God brought us together. I believe your purpose, my dear Nia, is to take my place here at The Puzzle House."

"Take your place? What do you mean?" But even as she said the words, her mind flashed to her puzzle, now on the wall downstairs. A picture of The Puzzle House with that perfect, beautiful rainbow. Was that God's promise to her?

"I believe God is giving you the same choice he gave me. To be a healer."

"A healer? No. He wouldn't do that. There's nothing special about me. I can't even pass biology. I'm a nobody."

"God doesn't create nobodies. We're all

special to Him."

"I'm not that special. Not like you are. It was enough that He chose to heal me. That's more than I deserved."

"Love isn't about deserving. It just is."

Tears streamed down Nia's cheeks. "Are you sure the doctors can't help —"

"I'm sure. But it's not about me right now. This is about you. I know you're young and you'll be faced with many decisions and choices that could lead you down a wrong path. I believe your path is my path. I believe in the gift God's given me. And to you." Rachel still held Nia's hand.

It was so warm. "I still don't understand why you think that I . . . I can ever be like you. That God would ever listen to me and answer my prayers. The way He does yours."

"Because you're an answer to my prayer. I know that. Whether you choose to continue the work here at The Puzzle House or go a different way. You have been given a gift. The gift of healing. But it's up to you to open it or not."

A healer? Could that really be true? A spark jumped to life inside her. Could she help other people? The way Rachel helped her and Brandon and so many others. "I could never be like you. As good and kind and patient as you are. I could never be like you."

"You don't have to be like me. God created you just the way he wanted you to be. He loves you just the way you are, my sweet Nia."

Nia closed her eyes and prayed. *Really, God. Is this true? You want me to be a healer?* As if in answer to her question, the hand Rachel held in her own tingled. The warmth, the peace spread from her fingers up through her arms and to the rest of her body.

Very softly, Rachel asked, "Do you feel it?"

"I feel it."

"God is here with us. He's asking you the same question He asked me long ago. Do you want to be a healer? Before you answer, know that it won't be an easy journey. In fact, it could be a difficult journey, but He will give you all you need for the trip."

Nia squeezed Rachel's hand. "I do. I want to help people. I want to be a healer."

"And I believe it will be so."

They sat together holding hands until the heat receded, but the peace remained.

Finally, Rachel smiled. "You should go get Cooper now."

"Now? It's time now?"

Rachel nodded.

"But there's so much I need to know. To learn. You have to teach me."

"Not me, God. You have all you need for the journey. Just remember the foundation. The frame."

"You mean God's Word."

She nodded. Her eyes fluttered. "I . . . need . . . Cooper."

Nia jumped off the bed and ran to the door. When she opened it, Cooper stood there along with other family members. Through tears, Nia managed to say, "She wants you." She stepped aside as the family filed in and turned to leave.

Cooper held out his hand. "Nia, don't go. We all want you here."

The others made agreeing sounds.

"But . . ."

"This is where you belong."

Nia took his hand. Her daughter placed a hand on Rachel's head. Jarrod placed his hand on her shoulder. The others did the same. When they were finished, each was holding someone's hand and touching Rachel.

"I love you, Grandma," Jarrod said.

"I love you, my beautiful grandson."

"Grandma, that's not what you say about boys."

Both of them smiled at the other.

Rachel's eyes fluttered open, and then shut for a time. Each time she opened them, she smiled at someone in the room. They would come close and she would whisper a special message to them, but Cooper's hand stayed in hers.

Finally, she looked at Cooper. "Thanks for . . . loving me."

"It's been my pleasure."

"I'll see you on the other side." She closed her eyes.

For a long time no one spoke.

Then Janet began to sing. "Amazing grace . . ."

The others joined in. When the song was finished, Rachel opened her eyes. She met Nia's gaze. "Don't . . . forget . . . about the love."

And then Rachel's eyes closed for the final time.

EPILOGUE

Five Years Later

Carrie Singleton stared out the windows of her car as she adjusted the turban on her bald head. She glanced at her husband driving.

He must have felt her gaze because he smiled at her.

"I think this is a mistake."

"You tell me that after we've driven six hours to get here?"

"Well, I didn't think so when we started out, but I think so now. The closer we get the more I think it's a mistake. There isn't anything anybody can do. The doctors said so."

"Sounds as if you're chickening out to me."

"Not really. Well, maybe. But why waste a week of my time here? I'd rather be with you, and I doubt anything miraculous will happen to me. I've prayed and prayed. And so have you. God's not listening to us anymore. Maybe it's time for us to accept . . . the inevitable."

Her husband shook his head. "What a person thinks is what a person becomes. You think no miracle so you get no miracle."

She held up her hand as if to ward off his words. "I know. I know. I've heard it all before. But really —"

"Too late now." Her husband turned into a drive. "We're here. And there's no way I'm turning around and driving back home with you in the car."

"It'll be a waste of money."

"They aren't charging a penny. It's supported by donations only. Remember?"

"And a waste of time."

"God is never a waste of time, my dear Carrie. At the very least, you'll have a nice, peaceful vacation. One you more than deserve."

Carrie looked at the scene before her.

A young woman led a beautiful brown and white horse around the pond with a child on it. The woman looked up as they drove closer to the house. She said something to the young boy on the horse. He slid off and then she handed him the reins. She walked over to them.

Carrie didn't get out of the car.

The girl came to her side. "Morning. Welcome to Puzzle House. I'm Nia."

"You're Nia. I didn't know you were so . . ."

"Young. I am." She shrugged.

"Thanks. But I've changed my mind. I don't —"

The girl opened Carrie's car door. "I know exactly what you're thinking."

"I doubt that very much."

She grinned at Carrie. "Sure, I do. You're thinking, what can this young, black girl teach an old, white lady like me. Right? Not that you're all that old, but you get what I mean. No offense meant."

Carrie chuckled. "I wouldn't have said it exactly like that. And no offense taken."

"But I'm pretty close?"

"I'm not that old."

"Very true. Sort of old compared to me, though. But as I said, I've been exactly where you are now."

"I doubt that."

"I was fifteen and the doctors told me there were no more treatments left to help me. That's when my Auntie brought me here. If I'd had the energy I'd have been kicking and screaming. But at the time I could barely walk." Nia leaned down and looped her arm through Carrie's. "You can always change your mind if you want. You've driven this far, might as well come in for a visit. So what brings you here?"

Carrie allowed herself to be pulled from the car by this beautiful young girl with such a sweet smile. "My husband."

"That's very funny, Carrie. Very funny. Is it OK for me to call you Carrie? Or I could call you Mrs. Singleton?"

"Carrie's fine. So do you think you'll heal me?"

"Only God heals, and there are many different ways to be healed, Carrie. That's between you and God." Arm in arm they walked toward the house. "All I'm here to do is to help you with your puzzle."

AUTHOR'S NOTE

Dear Reader,

Like Rachel. I was diagnosed with Neurofibromatosis Type 2 in the spring of 2012. It's been a difficult journey and it continues still. Unlike Rachel, I'd been studying God's Word for many years before I heard the words, "you have brain tumors."

1 Thessalonians 5: 16- 18 says, "rejoice always, pray continually, give thanks in all circumstances for this is God's will for you." Whenever I read these words as I took my journey, I would tell myself that I would give thanks in all circumstances but I would never be grateful for the circumstance of brain tumors.

However, Puzzle House would never have been written if I hadn't been diagnosed with brain tumors and NF2. So even though I still can't quite say that I'm thankful for the brain tumors, I can say that I'm thankful that I can use my experience to help others who may be suffering.

Just as healing comes in many different forms so does suffering. Like me you may be suffering physically, or you may have lost someone you love or a financial crisis or . . . The list can go on and on. But if you draw near to God, He will be there waiting for you.

That's His promise and I've found it to be true again and again.

I'm human and unlike Brandon, I've had more than my share of pity parties. But afterwards God gives me the strength to stand back up and keep moving forward. And He will do the same for you.

ABOUT THE AUTHOR

Lillian Duncan is a multi-published author who writes what she likes to read, mostly suspense and mystery. In 2012 she was diagnosed with Neurofibromatosis Type 2 as well as bilateral brain tumors.

As a retired speech pathologist, she believes in the power of words, especially God's Word.

The employees of Thorndike Press hope you have enjoyed this Large Print book. All our Thorndike, Wheeler, and Kennebec Large Print titles are designed for easy reading, and all our books are made to last. Other Thorndike Press Large Print books are available at your library, through selected bookstores, or directly from us.

For information about titles, please call:
(800) 223-1244

or visit our website at:
gale.com/thorndike

To share your comments, please write:

Publisher
Thorndike Press
10 Water St., Suite 310
Waterville, ME 04901